THE ASSERTIVE WOMAN

First Kim Kiley tried a smooth groin kick.

Remo moved aside as her leg went by, and caught her as she lost her balance.

She scratched at his face. He caught her nails in his palms and pressed her hands back to her sides.

She punched his chest. He let his chest muscles receive her knuckles and she let out a yell.

She punched again, this time at his head. Remo kissed the knuckles coming at him.

Remo figured the battle was over now. But he was wrong. The most beautiful and seductive woman in the world had just begun to fight. And if she couldn't defeat the Destroyer by attacking him, she would do it by surrendering. . . .

__ THE DESTROYER #62 __
THE SEVENTH STONE

62

The Destroyer

THE SEVENTH STONE

WARREN MURPHY & RICHARD SAPIR

A SIGNET BOOK

NEW AMERICAN LIBRARY

For Jessica and Michael.

Copyright© 1985 by Richard Sapir and Warren Murphy

SIGNET TRADEMARK REG. U.S. PAT. OFF. AND
FOREIGN COUNTRIES
REGISTERED TRADEMARK—MARCA REGISTRADA
HECHO EN CHICAGO, U.S.A.

SIGNET, SIGNET CLASSIC, MENTOR, PLUME, MERIDIAN and
NAL BOOKS are published by New American Library
1633 Broadway, New York, New York 10019

First Printing, August, 1985

1 2 3 4 5 6 7 8 9

PRINTED IN THE UNITED STATES OF AMERICA

Chapter One

Before there was an Out Island Spa owned by Del Ray Promotions, before there was a Bahamian government, before there was the black slave or the British colonizer, back when the little Out Islands were too small to bother with, even for the Carib Indians, and the beaches were truly—as centuries later, advertisements would say—"without footprints," there came to what would one day be known as Little Exuma Island a foot.

The foot was in a silver brocade slipper and before it touched the sandy beach a servant tried to place a gold carpet beneath it. The servant was waved away and so was the carpet as the royal feet were joined by others, wearing bronze and steel shin protectors.

They were the feet of soldiers and quickly they spread out, beyond the beach, into underbrush, scaring birds to flight and sending lizards scurrying to holes in the sparse white coral rocks.

Neither the birds nor the lizards had ever seen men before, least of all men with glistening chest-plates and helmets, swords at the ready and spears poking bushes and shaking the low-growing scrub trees.

On the beach, the prince shook off his slippers and pressed his bare feet into the pure white sand. He had never seen sand this white or a sea as turquoise blue before, and in the last few years he had seen many seas.

He looked back at his great royal barks, anchored in the sheltered cove, each with the single great sail, now only white, but once embroidered with the crossed swords of his royal family to proclaim its presence and powers.

But the crossed-swords crest had been shamefully unstitched years before on different seas as his men tried to disguise who he was. Even his standards had been removed from the prow of the boats and if his barks had not been so large, they could have belonged to any common merchant from any port in the world.

"Do you think here?" one of his lords asked the prince.

"Bring me the maps and my navigator."

The navigator was rowed from the main bark, wine-sotted and weeping. One of the noblemen readied his ivory-pommeled sword, sure that his prince would demand the navigator's head.

Two lords helped the weaving stricken man to stand. Another gathered the leather-bound tubes which held the maps. The iron breastplates and helmets, so good against arrow and spear, burned the flesh in this strange sun. By every lord's calculation, they knew it was winter, but there were no snows here, not even cold winds, just the burning sun and the scrub brush and that strange turquoise sea.

"The maps were useless, your Majesty," sobbed the navigator.

"Let us make sure of that," said the prince. The parchment maps, each protected by a thin wax coating, were laid out on the sand and held down by flat heavy swords at each corner. Some of the lords, seeing their passage on these maps, felt the anguish of lost homes and lost lands. They saw on the map the great city of Rome. They had been guests there of the great Augustus Caesar, emperor and god. They had been under his protection.

And of course his protection had been useless too.

On another map was the civilized China. They all remembered the courts of the Tang Dynasty. For an entire case of jewels, such as even the Tang emperor had never seen, they had been granted sanctuary within his palace walls.

But after just a few days, the Tang emperor had returned the jewels and told them to leave.

"Are you admitting, great Emperor, that you do not rule in your own courtyards?" their prince had asked. "For if you are afraid of one man—

any man—then you do not rule in your kingdom."

The Tang court was hushed at such effrontery to their emperor, but the emperor had only laughed.

"You believe that?" asked the emperor.

"I do," said the prince, righteously.

"You still believe that, after all that has happened to you?"

"I do."

"Then let me give you more wisdom, Prince, because your throne—which you do not sit on any longer—was once almost as grand as ours," said the emperor. "When it is cold, one is not a coward to put on furs. When it is hot, it does not take fear to put on a shade hat. A man can rule only what a man can rule. Otherwise, he winds up as some who are too prideful, fleeing from one kingdom to another, without a throne, without lands, like a beggar on a dusty road."

Angrily, the prince had responded. "If one man frightens you so much, my Emperor, then sit forever on your throne. At his indulgence and at his whim."

Now everyone in the court knew such an insult would call for beheading, but the emperor had smiled again and ever so softly said:

"Your life is not mine to take. I leave that to my friend who is your enemy."

And so the prince and his lords had left the court of the Tangs too. And now their helmets burned their flesh in the month the Romans called

January after the god Janus. Foot soldiers came back from the underbrush.

"He is not here, my lord," they called out.

A white-bellied gull cawed as it lowered itself to a piece of gray driftwood. They all waited for the orders to remove their burning helmets. There were two hundred men now. When they had started, there were fifteen thousand.

When they had started, they all expected to return to their prince's palace within a week or two. After all, it was only one man. And one man, of course, had his limits, hadn't he? Their prince was all-powerful, wasn't he?

And their prince was right. The man had to be shown that he was just a hireling, scarcely more worthy of respect than a carpenter or a jeweler or a physician. After all, what did that man do that a common soldier could not do?

What their prince had never told any of them was that he could have kept his kingdom for just a simple sack of gold, only a fraction of what the Tang emperor had refused from them or only a small part of what the Romans took as just a gift to provide brief sanctuary.

The prince could have paid. Indeed, he owed it. But Prince Wo had found that out only later, when it was too late.

He had hired, on the highest recommendations, an assassin reputed to be so good that his work was at an entirely different level from anything that had ever been seen before. The word was that this little village in the country known as Korea had provided assassins for centuries, but only now were they becoming really popular west of China and the backward and barbaric Japan.

"You have got to try one," said a courtier. "They are wonderful. No excuses. No reasons why they fail. They just don't fail."

At the time Prince Wo did have a problem. His brother was hungrily eyeing his throne and was also building an army, too large an army just to defend his limited lands. Yet Prince Wo could not kill him until he started an attack, and his brother was not ready to start an attack until he had a good chance of winning it.

A quandary which could best be solved by his brother's death, and what Prince Wo wanted was for his brother to die by unknown hands.

"I want no one to be able to point a finger to this throne and say we were responsible for our brother's death," he told the assassin when he finally arrived at Prince Wo's court.

"You may begin composing the funeral dirge, your Majesty," said the assassin with a very low bow.

But the next day, Prince Wo's brother died in a fall from one of the parapets of his castle and the prince dismissed the assassin, no longer needing his services.

"Your Majesty," said the assassin. "Your brother's death *was* my services."

"He fell," said Prince Wo.

"You said you did not wish to appear to be behind his death."

"His death was an accident. It was a sign of the gods that I should not be opposed on this earth. I do not pay assassins for a gift from the gods."

"Your Majesty, I come from a small village, a poor village which if it did not get the tributes given my services would starve. Should it become thought that these tributes did not have to be paid, not only those living today in my village would starve but so would those to come in the future. So, your Majesty, giving full obeisance to your glory, nevertheless, I insist that I be paid, and paid publicly."

"I rule here," said Prince Wo.

"And greatly," said the assassin. "But I must be paid."

Prince Wo flicked his fingers and guards came forward to remove the assassin who had the effrontery to use the word "must" in front of his royal highness.

But the assassin moved as smooth as a stream through their arms and without guidance left the throne room.

In the morning, the prince's favorite concubine was found dead from a fall. The court physician felt the bones and said that indeed she must have fallen a hundred feet. Yet she had been found lying on the floor alongside the king's bed.

The message was clear. There was not the slightest possibility that the prince's brother had

fallen accidentally. The assassin had sent his
message. He wanted to be paid.

Unfortunately, the entire court now knew what
had happened because falling from a bed and
breaking every bone in one's body was not something that could be kept secret, especially when it
was the prince's favorite concubine and it was the
prince's bed she fell from. They all knew now
what the prince knew. His brother had not died
by accident and the assassin had demanded
payment.

The prince sent a discreet courier to the assassin
with not only the payment, but double the payment. Inside the bag was a note:

"O Great Assassin. I cannot allow my throne to
be disgraced by seeming to be forced to pay you.
If I am forced to do anything, then how can I be
said to rule? Find double the agreed-upon
payment. The first part is for your service; the
second to kill the courier, keeping his silence and
yours."

The courier returned alive with the sacks empty
and with the assassin's demand. Payment must be
made to him publicly.

"Never," said Prince Wo. "If I am afraid of any
man in my kingdom, then I do not rule. He does."

He called his war council together and
explained what the problem was. The greatest
general among them pointed out that they were
used to fighting armies, not assassins. Each army

had its own special weakness. But none knew the weakness of this assassin.

The general devised what he called the seven-sided death. Each way of death would be inscribed on a stone. The first stone called for the sword; the second for poison; the third for treachery, and so on, until the seventh stone. If all the first six failed, then and only would the seventh stone be used.

"Why not use it first?" asked the prince.

Now the general was old and had fought many battles even before the prince was born. Unlike other warriors, he did not lead his men just by jumping on a horse before them, but was known to think. He would spend weeks and months alone, thinking about the ways of war, and while he was a frail man, he had never lost a battle. Even the most fearsome warriors bowed to the wisdom of his mind.

When he answered, he spoke slowly because everything he knew came from the work his mind had done.

"For every strength," he said, "there is a weakness. If the six ways fail, then the seventh will tell you the weakness of your enemy. The problem with most battles is that the general comes in with only one plan and if that fails, he fails. The seventh stone will be the invincible way, but must only be used should the other six fail."

*   *   *

As a precaution, the prince and his lords and his army moved out of the city into an encampment on a flat plain where no enemy could hide. Every soldier was issued a sword, for the sword was the way of the first stone. The general himself stood guard outside Prince Wo's tent.

In the morning, the general was found dead with every bone in his body broken.

The first stone was shattered and Prince Wo and his army and lords moved off into a valley where food was scarce. He ordered his men to poison every berry, every bush and well and grain, keeping their own foods safe, hidden inside their clothing. There they waited for the assassin, with the knowledge that in just a few days, he would be dead and they would be returning to the palace.

In the morning, Prince Wo's pet falcon was found dead at the base of his perch with every bone in his body broken.

Through the third, fourth, fifth, and sixth stones they fled. Baghdad, Rome, the land of the barbaric Scythians with strange yellow hair. Even the favorite mount of the Scythian king was killed in the same manner, every bone broken.

They were down to the last stone when Prince Wo with his remaining warriors ordered all the royal barks to provision and they sailed westward, carrying the stone sealed beneath his very bed. When they were a month out of sight of land, he ordered all the standards thrown overboard and the embroidered crossed swords on the sails removed, stitch by stitch, from existence.

It was then that the navigator began to weep and drink and could not be stopped. When finally they sailed into the turquoise-blue sea, the prince ordered the little fleet to anchor, and when it was shown no living thing was on the island, the prince ordered the navigator to come to shore with all the maps.

"Can anyone find this island or this sea?" Prince Wo asked.

"Your Majesty," weeped the navigator. "No one will ever find this island or this sea. We have sailed off the very maps of the world."

"Good," said the prince. "Bring the seventh stone and bury it here." He ordered the men to take off their burning helmets and throw them into the sea. When the stone, with its inscription on the seventh way to kill the assassin, arrived wrapped in silk, he ordered the ships to be burned where they were anchored.

"Your Majesty, why didn't you try the seventh way? Why didn't we at least try the seventh stone before we threw away our standards and shamefully removed the sign of the royal swords from your sails?"

Prince Wo said softly, "Is not the seventh stone the strongest way to overcome our enemy?"

"Then why not use it, your Majesty? Swords failed, poisons failed. The great pit near Rome

failed. Do you think, your Majesty, that the
seventh way will fail?"

"No," said Prince Wo and looked out on those
who had come with him so many thousands of
miles, who would never see the palace again. "It
will not fail. This will be the way to kill the
assassin. This was the way to be used when the
others failed. It is the most brilliant way."

"Why didn't we use it? Why didn't we use it
first?" he was asked.

Prince Wo smiled. "Would you all have come
with me, in boats shorn of emblems, with
standards surrendered to the sea like a retreating
navy? Would you have sailed willingly off the
maps of civilized men to an island like this where
we rule only birds and lizards? Would you have
done any of those things at the outset, willingly at
the outset?"

Everyone heard the waves, soft and steady,
breaking on the pure white beach.

"But, your Majesty. If we had tried the method
of the seventh stone, at the beginning, we would
not have had to flee."

Wo smiled again.

"Son," he said, addressing his subject warmly.
"This *is* the seventh way and I promise you will
destroy that house of assassins."

"When will he come?"

"Ah, that is the secret of the seventh stone,"
said the prince and kicked off his brocaded
slippers and wore only a cloth around his loins as

was most comfortable in this strange winter without snow.

Some thought that the summer would have snow, but it didn't. It got even hotter. Their skins browned and the years passed and wandering Carib Indians came and then the British and with them slaves to harvest the salt from flats flooded by the turquoise sea. And the islands became known as the Bahamas.

And one day, a steam shovel, cracking the coral ground for a condominium development, lifted up a smooth pink marble stone with engraving.

Shreds of tattered silk fell from it as it saw light for the first time in almost two thousand years. No one could make out the writing, not even the owner of Del Ray Promotions Inc. of Little Exuma.

"It ain't a curse, is it? Because if it's an old curse, then, you know, forget it already. It goes back in the ground. Screw the Indians." This from the major partner of Del Ray to the linguistics professor he had brought down from the States.

"No, no. It's nothing to do with Carib Indian. I would swear it's a form of Indo-European."

"We own this beachfront. It's ours. The Brits have been out of here for years."

"No. It's before the English language."

"Over a hundred years?" said the developer, who had never made it through high school and, as a form of compensation, liked to hire at least a dozen Ph.D's a year for various projects. Not for big money, of course. Big money was for his girl-friends and bigger money was for the private detectives who found out about it on behalf of his wife.

"Well over a thousand years," the professor said.

"What does it say?"

"I don't know. We may never be able to translate it."

There were, however, two people who translated it almost immediately. The sales manager for Del Ray said the stone promised peace, beautiful sunsets, and a resale value so unbelievable that only ancient Indo-European could describe it.

And Reginald Woburn III, called in by his father from a polo match to read the inscription on a photograph of the stone, did it too. Not as easily as the sales manager who was making up a sales pitch, but laboriously, step by step, picking his way carefully through the symbols of a language he had learned but never used. He sat in the dark polished room of the Woburn estate in Palm Beach and saw letters that he had learned as a child, when his father explained to him that the Jews had Hebrew, his Roman Catholic friends used to have Latin, and the Woburns had a language too.

"But, Daddy," Reginald had said. "Other

people use their languages. Nobody uses this language but the Woburns."

"And the Wolinskys. And von Wollochs and the de Wolliues and the Worths," his father had said.

"What sort of a language is that where you can only talk to a few hundred people?" Reginald had asked.

"Ours, son," his father had said. And since he was a Woburn and it was something his father had done and his father's father had done and everyone had done way back even before their name had become Woburn, Reginald Woburn III learned the language. Which was not too much to ask, considering that the rest of his life was to be spent in polo and bridge and yachting.

Now, in his prime, a full seven-goal polo player, Reginald was going through those old markings again.

It was gloomy in the main study. There was a reason for that. The light had to be filtered through dark windows. The rest of the world was sunny and gay and there were at least three delicious young ladies waiting for Reginald, and just as he did at twelve years of age, he picked laboriously through the letters.

Reginald was a darkly handsome young man in his twenties with high cheekbones and eyes that looked like black marbles. He was athletic but he never strained at it. When a coach had once told him, "No pain, no gain," Reginald had answered, "And no me."

This language had always been a nettling nuisance and he had hoped that it was something that was behind him. But here he was again.

He identified his verbs, his nouns, his proper nouns.

So typical of this language, the inscription on the stone included the word "stone." The language took the obvious and made it stupid. Not only was the inscription *on* the stone, it had to tell you it was on the stone.

"Seven times," said Reginald with his finger on the word in the photograph of the inscription.

"No," his father said. "Seventh stone."

"Right," Reginald said. "Seventh stone." He prayed that he was not going to have to read six others. He was getting thirsty but he knew one never allowed the servants around when you read the language.

There were six other stones, according to the inscription. The first was the stone of the sword and then the poison and so forth, through all manner of mayhem, including a pit somewhere.

Reginald looked up. Daddy was smiling. Therefore, Reginald could assume he was translating correctly. At least this was more interesting than most of the writings which had to do with the family of some Prince Wo and pithy little sayings like "If you fear someone, you never rule."

This inscription told about setting a trap, a trap

through history. It was a trap to kill someone named Sinanju.

"No. Not a person, a village," his father said.

"But it's a person sign here," said Reginald.

"Person or persons from Sinanju."

"Right," Reginald said wearily. "Person or persons from Sinanju. Kill them."

"Good," said his father. "Now you know what you have to do."

"Me? I'm a polo player."

"You're a Woburn. That inscription is your instruction."

"I've never killed anyone in my life," Reginald said.

"Then you can't be sure you won't like it."

"I'm sure I won't," Reginald said.

"You don't know if you don't try, Reggie."

"Isn't killing illegal?" Reginald asked.

"This thing you must do was written for us and for you before any laws of any country now existing on earth," said his father. "Besides, you're going to love it."

"How do you know?"

"Read on."

Reginald Woburn III picked his way through the lines of letters, seeing the thoughts become more intricate, seeing a stunning logic in a people disappearing from the face of the earth only to return in disguise to deliver the final and victorious blow.

It was sort of challenging in a way and even

though the other predictions of the stone had come true about how the island would be found by others and how Wo's descendants would move out disguised in the stream of humanity that came to the islands, Reginald could not quite believe the last prediction: that the first son of the first son of the direct line would, from a life of skilled idleness, become the greatest killer the world had ever known.

Of course, that would require eliminating all those who were the best now.

It was a game after all, Reginald reasoned. He did not know yet how much he was going to enjoy the blood of others.

Chapter Two

His name was Remo and he was going to make sure the man's children were on hand. With no other children would he ever do this, but this man had to see his children's faces looking at him. It was the way the man had killed. It had earned him this magnificent estate in Coral Gables, Florida, with the electrified Cyclone fence surrounding lawns like carpets on which sat, like some gross jewel, a magnificent white building with orange tile roof. It was a hacienda in America, built on needles and snorts and death, the death of children too.

Remo saw the television cameras pace their scans over the chain-link fence. Their mechanical rhythms were so steady, so dull, so avoidable. Why these people trusted technology instead of the native viciousness which had made them rich, Remo could not fathom. He waited, stock-still, until the camera caught him full face. Then he slowly moved a forefinger over his own throat and smiled. When the camera suddenly stopped and moved back to him and stayed on him, he smiled again and mouthed the words:

"You die."

That would do for openers. Then he went to the front gate where a large fat man sat in a booth, chewing something with enough garlic and peppers to fumigate the Colosseum at Rome.

"Hey, you. What you want?" said the man. He had a dark little mustache under his wide nose. His hair was thick and black like that of most Colombians. Even though he was just a guard at the gate, he was probably a brother or a cousin of the owner of the Coral Gables estate.

"I want to kill your patron and I want his children to see it," said Remo. He might have been mistaken for Indian himself with the high cheekbones and dark eyes. Yet his skin was pale. His nose was arrow straight and thin, as were his lips. Only his thick wrists might have drawn special attention. But the guard was not noticing the wrists. He had been told from the main house that a troublemaker was making strange signs at the cameras and he had been told to take care of him.

He was told to be reasonable. You asked nicely first, and then if the man didn't go, you broke his feet with a pipe. Then you called the police and an ambulance and they took him away. Maybe if he was real fresh, you broke his mouth too.

"Get outta here," said Gonzalez y Gonzalez y Gonzalez. That counted as the second warning. He was to give three. Gonzalez kept two fingers pressed against the little transmitter inside his booth. That way he wouldn't lose count. He had one more warning to go.

"No," said Remo.

"What?"

"I'm not going. I'm here to finish your patron," Remo said. "I am going to kill him and humiliate him. I've been told his children are here also."

"What?" grunted Gonzalez. It must be three by now. He reached for the man's neck. Suddenly his large hands left the transmitter and froze there in front of the man's neck. Gonzalez looked at his hands. The fingers he had been counting with were out there in midair. He had lost his place and now he wasn't sure if it had been three warnings or not.

"Hey, how many times I tell you to get out of here?" Gonzalez asked. Maybe the stranger would remember.

"I'm not leaving. I've got business with your patron."

"No, no," said Gonzalez. "I want to know exactly how many times I warned you to get outta here. What was it? One? Was it two?"

"I don't know," said Remo. "There was the first 'get outta here.' "

"Right. Thass one."

"I think there was another," Remo said.

"Okay. Three," Gonzalez said.

"No, that's two," Remo said.

"So you got one more."

"For what?" said Remo.

"For the three times I warn you before the surprise," said Gonzalez. He was being cunning. "Okay, here comes the third. Get you ass outta here before I break you feet."

"No," said Remo. Gonzalez went for the hammer. He liked to hear bones break, liked to feel them give way to a good solid swing. Gonzalez reached his free hand to grab the insolent stranger while he swung the hammer toward the groin. There was a strange light feeling to the hand that gripped the stranger and that was because it wasn't gripping anything anymore. It was gone, and the stranger didn't seem to move.

But Gonzalez's left arm ended at a gushing stump. Then the window shield of his guard booth closed and the door opened and he saw where his hand had gone. It came flying back into his lap.

He had not seen the stranger move because the other movement was so perfectly symmetrical with his own. He had only seen the hammer. He could not perceive an incredible velocity from the stranger's hand, cutting through his wrist like a scissor separating breakfast sausage, severing bone from bone with such awesome speed that Gonzalez did not even have time to feel pain.

There was only the lightness, and then the hand in his lap, and then everything became dark forever. He did not see the finishing blow to his head. His last thought was a stunning clear vision of reality. He saw a vision of a transmitter in front of his eyes. He saw two fingers on it. He was at two. That was his place. Two warnings. He would remember that if the subject came up again.

It didn't.

Remo felt the dogs before he heard them or saw them. There was a way dogs had about them of being unleashed for an attack. Dogs were pack animals, and while they could be trained for other things, they worked best in groups. On the other hand, man had to be trained to work in a group. And then there were a few other men, down through the centuries, who had been trained to excel alone, to use all the physical powers that a man's body could command, and those were the ones who could sense dogs loping across a vast lawn preparing for an attack.

Remo was one of those men. The only other was his trainer, and Remo's training had been so pure that he no longer had to think about the things he knew. To think about something was not to know it. To do something without knowing how one did it was the full knowledge of one's own body.

The normal human body would tense when perceiving an attack. That was because it had

succumbed to the bad habit of using muscles and
strength. When the dogs set forepaws for the leap,
Remo felt a softness in the air, almost as if
watching himself. He let his left arm level out by
itself with palm upward, catching the underbelly
of the dog and pressuring slightly so that its leap
went two feet too far, two feet above his head. He
passed the other two dogs, one at each side, like a
matador.

From the window of the great white house with
the orange roof, a man watched through
binoculars. He rubbed the lenses because he was
sure he had not seen what he had seen. If his
binoculars were not playing tricks, he had just
seen his three prize attack dogs leap at a man and
not only miss, but seem to go right through him.
The man did not change pace; nor did he change
expression.

There was Lobo, Rafael and Berserka, each
with a blood kill in their mouths by the time their
training had been completed, and they had run
through that stranger.

Was he carrying something special?

What could he carry? He wore only a black
T-shirt and black slacks and loafers. He also wore
a smile. Apparently he knew he was being
watched because he mouthed again the words:

"You're dead."

Lobo pulled up short on the lawn and, true to
his great Doberman heart, whirled to attack
again. And this time it was as if he had run into a

wall. He stopped. Flat. On the ground. Lifeless.

A useless dog, thought the man with the binoculars. Rafael would do better. Rafael had once ripped out a lumberjack's throat with one jerk of his mastiff neck.

Rafael roared toward the man's groin. Rafael roared right on by in two pieces. Mastiff's master watched his dog die and thought: "All my life, I have been robbed by dog dealers. Let there be one day that does not betray Juan Valdez Garcia and then I will admit there is justice under heaven."

Juan Valdez prayed rarely and never without some prospect of success. He was not a man who would ask a favor of the Almighty without believing it was in the Almighty's best interest to deliver. Juan Valdez was not, after all, some pathetic peasant who would ask for the impossible, like altering an incurable disease.

Juan allowed the Almighty a likely opportunity to perform this service for him. After all, had he not twice placed gold candlesticks in the churches of Bogota and Popayan? He was not a man to treat God to mere copper.

Having paid for services, Juan Valdez now expected those services to be returned. It was a simple prayer that came from his lips, one that was honest and true:

"God, I want that gringo in Berserka's teeth. Or else I calling in the candlesticks."

Juan focused the binoculars a bit more tightly. It would be good to see Berserka kill. She did not finish off quickly, unlike his other dogs, who went for the throat. Berserka could kill like a cat when she had a person helpless. Berserka, who had once shredded two men with rifles and sent a third fleeing handless into the jungles in Juan's early days of harvesting coca leaf, now darted toward the gringo's ankle. Berserka had teeth like a shark and haunches like a rhino. Her paws dug up lawn as she drove toward the man's loafers. And then she twisted with the full weight of her body to jerk him off his feet.

But she was twisting in air, a 180-pound dog bouncing around in the man's hands like a puppy. And he was stroking her belly and he was saying something Juan Valdez made out by lip-reading.

He was saying: "Nice doggy."

And then he put her down and she walked, tail wagging behind the heels she was supposed to have upended. Juan gasped. There was Berserka, who had chewed on more entrails than he could count, happily walking behind this man who had invaded his home. Juan did not care anymore where he was. It was his home. So what if it was in America? It was his home and the machine guns would have to be used.

But his cousins protested. A machine gun might hit neighboring estates. A machine gun might carry shells to a hospital a mile down the road. A machine gun could do damage anywhere. Why did Juan wish to use machine guns in an American suburb?

"Because I couldn't lay my hands on an autmic bomb, *estupido*," he said and personally supervised the setting up of the fifty-caliber machine guns.

The deadly spray chewed up his lawn, pulverized his beloved Berserka and left the man unscathed. He was unscathed, Juan was sure, because he wasn't there anymore. Like a mist that suddenly goes when the sun arrives, he was gone. And then he was at the window, without a mark on him.

Juan Valdez would never trust the Lord again. The Almighty deserved all those windows' mites he kept asking for. If Juan lived through this day, he would take back the gold candlesticks from the churches in Bogota and Popayan.

His stupid cousins were still firing the machine guns into the expensive lawn when the man spoke.

"I've come to see Juan Valdez," said Remo.

Juan pointed to his stupid cousins.

"Which one is Juan Valdez?" Remo asked.

"They both are. Take them with my blessings and go," said Juan.

"I think you are."

"You're right," said Juan. He had not expected that to work. What could he say to a man who had killed his gate guard, destroyed his two favorite dogs personally and the third practically, and was now cracking the bones of his cousins as if they were lobsters?

New words came easily to Juan Valdez and they were sincere.

"Stranger, I don't know who you are but you're hired."

"I don't work for dead men," said Remo and grabbed Valdez by the back of his neck, pressing the thick greasy hair into the skin. Juan saw darkness and felt pain and when the gringo asked for his children, he heard himself to his own surprise answering.

Valdez was dragged like a sack of coffee beans into the children's room, where the German governess was dismissed.

There were Chico and Paco and Napoleon.

"Children," said the gringo. "This is your father. He has helped to bring a new form of death to America's shores. Your father doesn't believe in just killing witnesses; he kills their wives and children. That is how your father kills."

Even as he said this, Remo felt the same rage he had felt when he heard that ten children and their mothers were slain in New York City in a dispute between drug dealers. Remo had seen killing in the world, but not like this. Children had died in wars, but to use them as precise targets made his blood run cold and when he got this assignment, he knew exactly what he was going to do.

"Do you believe that children should be killed in these drug wars?"

Their little dark eyes grew larger with fear. They shook their heads.

"Don't you think that people who kill children are *mierda*?" Remo asked, using the Spanish word for excrement.

They all nodded.

"Your daddy kills children. What do you think he is?" And even as the first frightened hesitant answers came from their lips, Remo finished off Valdez, wiping his hands clean on the man's shirt. And there were the children looking at their father, whose last vision on earth had been that of his children saying he was less than dirt.

And Remo felt unclean. Why had he done it like that? He was just supposed to eliminate Valdez and he felt unclean now.

He looked at the children and said, "I'm sorry."

What was he sorry about? His country and the world were infinitely better off with this man's death. Valdez, by his brutality, his slaughtering of the families of witnesses, had remained free from the law. And this was Remo's job. When the nation was threatened by those who could not be contained within the law, then the organization he worked for took care of things outside the law.

And he had done it. Almost as ordered. But no one had ordered him to kill a man in front of his children. And there was something worse: he had unleashed all the old feelings he had grown up with, all the feelings he had been trained out of.

"I'm sorry," Remo repeated.

"Hey," said the oldest boy, the one called Napoleon. "That's the business, baby. At least you didn't kill the children. Let's hear it for the handsome gringo."

The two other boys started to applaud.

"And on your way out, kind gringo, would you please take Daddy? They tend to smell up the place after a while."

"Sure," said Remo.

The kid had a nice way of looking at things. Maybe Remo's feelings were just a brief throwback to his days before training. This anger surprised him, though. He wasn't supposed to feel anger anymore, just a unity with all the forces that made him work correctly.

Then why was he worried? He had nothing to worry about. Just a feeling, and feelings didn't kill people. Of course, other people weren't so finely tuned that even their emotions were expected to be synchronized with their movements and their breathing and their being. It was almost like a golfer who, if he finished in a wrong position, knew—even without looking—that he had hit the ball wrong.

But, Remo told himself, nothing had gone wrong. Therefore, nothing *was* wrong.

And besides, only he had to know about it.

Nothing was wrong.

Halfway across the country, the last Master of Sinanju, sun source of all the martial arts and defender of the Korean village of Sinanju, knew something was wrong, and he waited for Remo to return.

Chiun, the Master of Sinanju, was in the American city of Dayton in the state of Ohio. Dayton looked to Chiun just like all other American cities with green signs and fine highways, just like Rome in the time of the Great Wang, the greatest of all Masters of Sinanju. Chiun had often told Remo about the similarities between serving Rome, as did the Great Wang, and serving America.

Of course, in the histories of Sinanju, nothing was quite so strange as this country which had given birth to Remo.

As Master, it was Chiun's responsibility to pass on the history of his masterhood, just as it would someday be Remo's responsibility.

Chiun would not lie in writing the history of his reign because that would be dangerous to other Masters who would follow and carry out the work as great assassins to the world. But he did not necessarily, when writing his histories, include all the facts. Such as the fact that Remo was not only *not* born in Sinanju, and was not only *not* Korean, but he was not even Oriental. He was a white and therein was the problem. Remo had been raised white, taught white and lived among whites until Chiun had gotten him with more then twenty-five years of bad habits ingrained in him.

In the many centuries of the assassins of

Sinanju, each Master faced an occasional time in which all that he had been trained to be would recede, only to blossom fully again. A Master who had been raised in the village of Sinanju could deal with this because, as a Korean child, he had been taught the game of hide.

All the children of Sinanju knew that every so often a Master would return to his house and not again cross the threshold for a long time. He would stay there and it was the task of the village to tell everyone he had left and was off serving some other emperor or king.

It was the game called hide. And every Sinanju-trained Master knew that when his powers were less and he had descended from peak, he must hide and remove himself from service until it passed.

But what would Remo know? What would he remember? What white games were there to tell him what to do? Would he remember where he was raised in that white Catholic orphanage? What games could the Church of Rome teach Remo that would prepare him for the moment of coming down from his peak?

How could he know that in feeling again old feelings that he had thought were buried he was being given a signal to hide, to retreat like a wounded animal until he was well again?

These were the questions the Master of Sinanju, in Dayton, Ohio, United States, asked himself. Because he knew Remo's problem. He had seen the signs in Remo even though Remo hadn't yet seen them. Oddly enough, the trouble began when one felt perfection, a total unity of mind and thought and body.

Remo had been happy before he left and Chiun had criticized him for it.

"What's wrong with feeling perfect, Little Father?" Remo had said.

"To feel perfect can be a lie," Chiun had said.

"Not when you know it's so," Remo said.

"From what place is the most dangerous fall?" asked Chiun.

"I know what bothers you, Little Father. I'm happy."

"Why shouldn't you be? You have been given everything of Sinanju."

"So what is there to worry about?" Remo had asked.

"You have not been given birth in Sinanju."

"My eyes are always going to be round," Remo said.

But it was not the eyes. It was the childhood, and Chiun had not given so many years of his life to see it wasted now because of an accident of birth. He knew what to do. He would use the American telephone. Even if Remo didn't know it, Chiun knew it. Remo was in trouble.

Chiun's movements were like molten glass, slow but with a sureness of flow that transcended the normal jerky movements of men. His long fingernails stretched from a golden kimono reaching for the black plastic thing on the hotel-room table, the thing with the buttons. He had parchment-frail skin and wisps of white hair hung down over his ears. He looked elderly, as old as sand, but his eyes danced like a falcon on the soar.

From his robe he took the proper codes that worked the thing that Americans placed all over their country. Their telephones. He was going to work one. He was going to save Remo from himself.

He did not even try to assume the essence of the instrument. He had tried that before, several times, and feeling nothing, sensing nothing, let it be. But now, this was the only way to reach Emperor Smith, a white who was always as remote as a faraway wall. He was a man, Chiun truly believed, who was filled with a plan to seize the country and the plan was either brilliant or sheer lunacy.

Remo, in his innocence, continually assured Chiun that Smith had no plan for national takeover. First, he said, Smith was not an emperor. He was simply Dr. Harold W. Smith. Second, Remo said, both Smith and Remo worked for an organization they wanted no one to know about. This organization enabled the government to work and enabled the country to survive by working outside the Constitution against the country's enemies.

Remo even showed Chiun a copy of that

document once. Chiun had admitted it was truly beautiful with all its rights and protections, all its many ways of doing things to exalt its citizens.

"Do you pray this often?" Chiun had said.

"It's not a prayer. It's our basic social contract."

"I do not see your signature, Remo, unless of course you are really John Hancock."

"No, of course I'm not."

"Are you Thomas Jefferson?" Chiun asked.

"No. They're dead," Remo said.

"Well, if you didn't sign it and Emperor Smith didn't sign it and most people did not sign it, how can it be a basic social contract?"

"Because it is. And it's beautiful. It's what my country is about, the country that pays Sinanju for your services in training me."

"They could not pay me for what I have taught you," Chiun said.

"Well, it's who I serve. And who Smitty serves. Do you understand?"

"Of course. But when do we remove the current President for Emperor Smith?"

"He is not an emperor. He serves the President."

"Then when do we remove the President's opponent?" Chiun asked, truly trying to understand.

"We don't. The people do. They vote. They vote who they want to be President."

"Then why have an assassin with the power to remove a President or keep him in office?" Chiun had asked.

Confronted by absolute logic, Remo had given up and Chiun had copied the Constitution into the history of the House of Sinanju so that perhaps, one day in the future generation, someone in Sinanju would figure out what these people were up to.

Now on the American instrument, Chiun was reaching out for Emperor Smith. With these devices, the person speaking could be anywhere. The next room or across the continent. But Chiun knew that Emperor Smith ruled from a place in the state of New York called Rye, and often from an island called St. Maarten in the Caribbean. When he was there, Chiun often wondered if he had been sent into exile or was waiting for the President to be removed from the throne, a service Sinanju would provide on request.

Chiun carefully pressed the numbered code into the machine. The machine spoke back with little bipping gurgles. There were many numbers. There were many bips. One mistake, one number wrongly inserted, a six instead of a seven and the machine would not work.

Somehow in this country, even the children of these ungainly and ugly people seemed able to operate these number codes to speak to other ungainly and ugly people.

As Emperor Smith had explained, the numbers

that he gave Chiun would activate another machine that would not let people listen in. How wise that was, especially for a fool who if he did not act soon against the President, would be too old to enjoy the pleasures of the throne.

Suddenly there was a ringing on the other end. And the voice that answered was that of Smith. Chiun had done it. He had mastered the machine with the codes, the codes of the Americans.

"I have done it," Chiun said in triumph.

"Yes, you have, Master of Sinanju. What can I do for you?" Smith asked.

"We have great dangers, O wise Emperor."

"What's the problem?"

"There are times when Remo is at his height. And times when he is not, when he is low. Never so low that he is a bad product; that I can assure you. But I am looking out for your longer-term interest, Emperor Smith."

"What are you saying?"

"Not that you will not be protected. I will always be here for you. Your tributes to Sinanju are sufficient and do glory to your name."

"I am not increasing the payments," Smith said. "As you know, we have enough difficulty smuggling them into Sinanju as it is. The submarine trips are almost as costly as the gold."

"May my tongue wither, O Emperor, if I ask for another payment beyond your generosity," said Chiun, making a mental note to remind Smith at the next negotiation that if the delivery cost was almost as much as the tribute itself, then the tribute was obviously too small.

"Then what is it?" Smith asked.

"To further enhance your safety, may I suggest that Remo perform in the traditional manner of all Masters of Sinanju. That is to do more when he is at the level of perfection and to do less at times when your glory would be less well served."

"Are you saying that Remo should take some time off? Because if you are, you won't have a problem here," Smith said.

"How wise," said Chiun, ready with a counter-argument should Smith suggest that payments be accordingly reduced. Yet in his inscrutability, Smith said nothing of the sort. He said that Remo deserved a vacation and should take a rest.

"Please be so kind, most enlightened Emperor, to come here to Dayton of Ohio and tell this to Remo yourself."

"You can tell him," Smith said.

Chiun allowed a deep sigh. "He will not listen to me."

"But you're his teacher. You taught him everything."

"Ah, the bitter truth of that," said Chiun. "I taught him all but gratitude."

"And he won't listen to you?"

"Can you imagine? Nothing. He listens to nothing I say. I am not one to complain, as you well know. What do I ask of him? Some concern. To keep in touch. Is that a crime? Should I be ignored like some old shoe whom he has worn out?"

"Are you sure that Remo feels that way? I know that he defends you at every turn," Smith said. "I am happy with your service but sometimes we have disagreements and Remo always takes your position. He used to agree with me more."

"Really?" said Chiun. "How have you been attacking me?"

"I haven't. We have had different positions occasionally though."

"Of course," said Chiun. He would have to question Remo about this and find out how Smith had been attacking him. "I ask that you personally tell Remo to rest."

"All right, if you think that's wise."

"Most wise, O Emperor, and if you would confide in me how the position of Sinanju in any way differs from the wonders of your line of correct thought, we will adjust ourselves to your slightest whim."

"Well, there's this problem with your seeking outside work, possibly for tyrants and dictators. . . ."

Chiun let the receiver fall on the two buttons of the cradle. He had seen Remo do that when he wanted to stop talking to someone and it seemed to end the conversation very nicely.

When the telephone rang again, Chiun did not pick it up.

*   *   *

When Remo returned from Coral Gables to the hotel room in Dayton, Ohio, he saw that Harold W. Smith was waiting there for him, along with Chiun.

He wondered if Smith ever changed the style of his suit. Gray, three-piece, Dartmouth tie, white shirt, and acid expression.

"Remo, I think you should take a vacation," Smith said.

"Have you been talking to Chiun?"

And in Korean from another room came Chiun's squeaky voice: "You see? Even a white recognizes the fact of your cosmic separations."

And in Korean, Remo answered back:

"Smitty has never heard of a cosmic separation. Nothing is wrong with me and I'm not taking a vacation."

"You defy your emperor?" Chiun said.

"I don't want to be maneuvered into a vacation by you, Little Father. If you want me to take a vacation, just say so."

"Take a vacation," Chiun said.

"No."

"You said to say so," Chiun said.

"I didn't say I'd do it," Remo said. "I'm fine."

"You're not fine. You only feel fine," Chiun said.

Harold W. Smith sat rigidly in a chair, listening to teacher and pupil, Smith's sole enforcement arm for the entire organization called CURE, argue in a language that he did not understand.

"Remo," said Smith finally. "It's an order. If Chiun thinks you ought to rest, you ought to rest."

"He also thinks we ought to kill the President and make you President so that he has something of value to show for his time here. Should I do that?"

"Remo, you always turn on the people who care about you," said Chiun.

"I'm not taking a vacation."

"There really is nothing of danger now, no emergency. Why don't you just take a little rest?" said Smith.

"Why don't you mind your business?" Remo asked.

"You are my business," Smith said.

Remo let out a little whistle, something vaguely like a Walt Disney tune, picked up Smith in his chair and put the chair and Smith out in the hallway.

Smith looked back and said simply:

"Are you telling me you don't need a rest, Remo?"

Remo looked at Chiun, contentedly folding his arms into his kimono.

"Where do you suggest?"

"I don't want you in continental America. What about the Caribbean?" Smith said.

"St. Maarten?" Remo asked.

"No. Too close to our computer backup in Grand Case harbor. What about the Bahamas? There's a condo development in Little Exuma.

Take a rest there. You've always wanted a home. Buy a condo," Smith said. "A cheap one."

"I wanted a home in an American town, on an American street, with an American family," Remo said bitterly.

"This is what we can give you for now, Remo. But you should know that what you're doing is helping other Americans have that dream."

"Maybe," said Remo. "I'm sorry about putting you in the hall. But I really am feeling fine."

"Sure," said Smith.

"I am," said Remo to Chiun. And even Chiun agreed, but no one believed him, not even himself anymore.

Chapter Three

A Korean had come to Little Exuma Island, to the new Del Ray condominiums. He was one of the first buyers of a condominium unit. A Korean, in Korean robes.

"All right, Dad," said Reginald Woburn III. "I'll get to it. I'll get to it."

"When? He's already there, right where the stone was uncovered. The forces of the cosmos are with us. Now is the time for revenge. Now is the time to strike at the one our ancestors were defenseless against."

"You mean a Korean coming to where our supposed ancestor buried the stone of the seventh way? Do you know how many Koreans there are in the world? Do you know the odds against that particular Korean being a descendant of that assassin, who should have been paid to begin with?"

"Reggie, no more excuses. It's your duty to the family."

"I don't believe this Korean is anyone special," Reginald said.

"Do you believe in getting your allowance?"

"Devoutly, Father."

"Then at least begin. Show the rest of the family you are doing something."

"What?"

"Something," his father said.

"You mean start taking potshots at every Korean who walks in the street?"

"What's bothering you?" his father said.

"I don't want to kill anyone. That's bothering me. I do not want to take a life."

"Have you ever killed anyone?" asked Reginald's father. He sat facing the young man on the spacious white veranda in the Palm Beach home. The young man didn't quite know what it was like to deal with the rest of the family.

"Of course not," Reginald answered.

"Then how do you know you wouldn't like it?"

"Really, Father. I will do it. I just need more time. It's like a game with proper moments for things and now isn't the proper time. I am the chosen one, according to the stone. I am supposed to be the most ferocious of all in my lust for blood. Now, Father, I know about lust. And I know you can't force it."

He swirled the remnants of his sweet iced drink and took the last sip. He hated these talks about the family because the servants were never allowed near enough to hear and that meant you could never get anything to drink if you needed it. It was good being part of the family, Reggie knew, because if one weren't, one might have an excellent chance of being poor or having to work, neither of which appealed to him. The bad thing was that the family tended to get a bit bonkers when it got onto itself. Like this stupid stone. Everything depended on the stars, which were the clocks of the universe. And at that right time, the family would produce its great blood-lust killer. And now it was supposed to be him. Ridiculous. As if all the family genes were bubbling away toward the purpose of a two-thousand-year-old revenge. Reggie had no use for revenge. You couldn't drink it, sniff it or make love to it. And you probably got overheated in the process. But Father appeared insistent. He just wasn't going to stop and Reggie knew he was not going to be able to wait him out.

"Try killing a small thing. See how you feel then. Just a small thing," his father said.

"I swatted a fly this morning. It did nothing for me, Father."

"Kill a little thing. Just so the family will see you are doing something."

"How little?"

"Warm-blooded," his father said.

"I'm not going to harm some defenseless puppy somewhere."

"Game. A game animal, Reggie."

"All right. We'll have to plan something."

"A safari," said his father.

"Excellent," said Reginald Woburn III, knowing that a good safari sometimes took a year to plan and in that time he might get himself injured in polo or the stone might blow up or something or that poor Korean might die of a heart attack or be hit by a car—anything to get this family-legend thing off his back. "A safari. Wonderful."

"Good," said his father. "The jet's engines are warming. It's been ready for takeoff all morning."

Fortunately, there was Dom Perignon on the private jet but unfortunately there was this white-hunter type talking about guns and kills and saying what good sport it was all going to be.

The first thing about Zaire, other than the stench of human waste in the capital city, was that it was extraordinarily hot, Reggie noticed. And worse, there was no way to hunt elephants from an air-conditioned van. It was considered unsporting. The second thing about Zaire was that the best trackers were Pygmies, little black Africans who were at an even lower social scale than the dirt-poor starving farmers.

Reginald Woburn III saw some elephants at a distance from his Land Rover, saw lions, saw zebras, and would have preferred to see them all in the Bronx Zoo because that was a half-hour from Manhattan, whereas Zaire was a day by jet.

Then the little trackers, downwind from the elephants but unfortunately upwind from Reginald Woburn III, started to run.

"Come. Run. We'll lose them," said the white hunter. He wore one of those khaki hunting jackets with places for big shells, and polished boots and a ridiculous wide-brimmed hat with some leopard band around it. He was running too.

"We can always follow the scent," said Reginald, who could barely move through the underbrush, much less run.

"Watch your rifle. Hold it down. You can set that thing off," said the white hunter. His name was Rafe Stokes, he drank warm Scotch, smoked a pipe and had talked incessantly the night before about a good kill. Reggie had thought that the only good kill would have been by a can of bug killer. The insects were all over the place.

Rafe Stokes, great white hunter, had talked so unendingly about the elephant as a friend, its nobility, its strength, its loyalty, Reggie had wondered if they were actually going to kill the beast or paint a medal on its smelly side.

Reggie knew that there had to be more about elephants, something unpleasant. He found out that hot day stumbling through the Zaire brush. The largest gooiest thing in the world was an elephant dropping. It was the size of a round lawn table. It was a fresh dropping, Reginald knew, because it felt warm around his knees.

Even after that, Reggie didn't want to kill an elephant. He just wanted to wash. He wanted to cut off his clothes and swim in lye for a week.

Finally Rafe Stokes, great white hunter, signaled Reggie to stop. Now Reggie didn't want to stop. He wanted to run upwind from himself. But there he stood, with flies buzzing around, his leg warm and gooey to the knee, waiting for the hunter to tell him to shoot. He would shoot, he would go home and possibly delay the family for a year. Hopefully, he might even break a leg on this safari and make it two years.

The hunter pointed. There, less than a hundred yards away, was a massive building with legs and trunk and tusks. Its ears were big enough for awnings. Great whitish swashes like camouflage coated the thick gray skin. It had rolled in mud, the white hunter had said. Elephants were good at that. They were also good at overturning cars, trampling people into goo, and hurling persons through the air like peanuts.

Good reason to avoid them, Reggie had thought, when being told all this lore. He hated lore. Jungle lore was another phrase for elephant droppings. If it had any truth to it, they wouldn't call it lore, they would call it information.

"Go ahead, he's yours," whispered the white hunter. The Pygmies stood nearby grinning, looking at Reggie, loooking at the elephant.

Reggie sighted the middle of the thing between the V and the post of the sights.

Some sport, he thought. He'd have to strain his neck to miss that monster.

"Shoot," whispered the white hunter.

"I will," said Reggie. "Just leave me alone."

"He's getting ugly," said Rafe Stokes.

"Getting?" said Reggie. The little black people were starting to edge back into the brush. The elephant turned.

"The whole thing is ugly," Reggie said.

"Shoot," said Rafe Stokes, raising his own gun. But still he waited. Reggie Woburn's father had warned Stokes that his son had to taste blood. If the hunter shot the beast, he would not be paid. Strange old coot, too. Didn't want the trophy. As the old saying went, the apple never fell far from the tree. Both of these Woburns were fruits.

The father had assured Rafe Stokes, twenty-eight years in the brush, never lost a hunter yet, that the son would be the most marvelous hunter he had ever seen. Now, with the bull elephant roaring down on them like a house sliding down a hill, making the very gound tremble, Rafe was one trigger pull away from not collecting the rest of his fee.

And then it happened. A shot went into the elephant's right-front kneecap. The fruitcake had missed, sending the bull elephant rolling toward them, crushing trees under its body. They sounded like little firecrackers going off as their trunks coughed up splinters at the sever point.

Crack, crack, crack. And then the elephant's testicles exploded between its legs. The tenderfoot had missed a kill shot again as the hulk of the screaming beast rolled toward them, leaving a carpet of snapped trees and pressed bushes.

The tenderfoot was reloading. He missed again, getting another knee. The elephant stopped rolling just in time and tried to rise but its front knees had been shot out. And then its trunk went from the powerful blast of the 447 Magnum rifle.

The poor bastard screamed in agony.

"Finish it, dammit," the hunter yelled to Reggie. "Just point to the head and shoot. Shoot, dammit."

Rafe was pushing his rifle into the tenderfoot's hands. Use this, use this. Slowly, with measured pace, Reginald Woburn III took the elephant gun in his hands and felt the tooling of the stock and smiled at the sweating desperate white hunter.

The elephant screams were a tingle in Reggie's ears, like music he had heard once in Tangiers when he was given the best hashish in the country and he heard a note for what must have been a half-hour. An illusion, of course, but an ultimate pleasure too.

"I will finish it when I am ready," said Reginald. And then, very casually, shot off an ear piece by piece. It took four shells. They were big ears.

"You can't do this," screamed the white hunter. "You've got to finish your kill."

"I will. In my own way," said Reginald Woburn III. A great peace was on him now as the beast bellowed in pain. Reggie no longer minded the smell of his boots or the flies or the jungle because he had experienced that one great note of life and knew now what he should do. The white hunter's agony added to his joy.

"I'm going to finish it," said the hunter, snatching back his rifle. He jerked the gun to his shoulder and with one motion put a bullet through the elephant's eye.

Then he turned away from his client and let out a deep disgusted sigh.

"That was my kill," said Reggie. "Mine."

The hunter did not turn to look. "You have no right, Mr. Woburn, to torture the game. Just to kill it."

"My rights are what I say they are."

"Sonny, this is the brush. If you want to get back alive, you'll keep your mouth shut."

"No, thank you," said Reggie, who now understood why his ancestor had been unable to publicly pay the assassin. "I just can't allow that. You see, there are things I can allow and things I cannot. You just cannot talk to me like that. And most of all, you cannot take away my kill no matter how your sensitivities are bruised. Do you understand?"

Perhaps it was the softness of the voice, so strange after such a brutal kill. Perhaps it was the quiet of the brush, as if a great killer now stalked through it, but Rafe Stokes, white hunter, loaded his gun again, keeping it tight by his body. This tenderfoot is going to kill me, he thought. He had a gun and he was standing behind Stokes. Was it loaded? Had he fired off all his shots? Stokes didn't know why for certain, but years of hunting had taught him when he was in real danger and he was in real danger now.

He planted a foot and very slowly, with the gun ready, he turned. And there was Reginald Woburn III, smiling as foppishly as ever, trying to clean off his clothes.

"Oh, c'mon," said Reggie. "You're so serious. Don't take me so seriously, for God's sake. We'll tell Dad I shot the beast and you'll get your money and I will get my family off my back for a while. All right?"

"Sure," said Rafe, wondering how he could have been so wrong. That night, he had a drink with his client, toasted the hunt even though the head was too shot up for a good trophy, toasted the Pygmies and toasted Africa, which Reggie assured everyone he was never going to visit again.

Rafe Stokes went to his tent for the best night's

sleep he ever had. It never ended. Just after the hunter began to snore, Reggie went into his tent with a dinner knife and sawed through his throat, then buried the blade in his heart.

It was delicious. Just as they were getting back to civilization, Reggie realized he didn't need the Pygmies anymore to guide him to the airport. So he took them as little snacks, popping their heads open with a pistol. If you hit them in the back of their heads, he realized, you could get the brains to fly out like a bowl of oatmeal getting a shot put plopped into it. Delicious. It was better than polo, better than cooling drinks on white verandas, better than the great summer balls of Newport, better than hashish in Tangiers. Better than sex.

It was what he had been born to do.

His father knew instantly that the change had occurred.

"Your highness," he said.

Reggie put out his right hand, palm down, and his father fell to one knee and kissed it.

"It would be fortunate if this Korean is the right Korean," said Reggie. "But we are going to have to make certain."

In his newfound wisdom, he had understood the seventh stone. One had to use time. That was what the years had given them. Time.

First they would find out if the Korean was the one, and then they would use all the years of hiding to perform the one way that would have to kill him. It was right and just. A king should never bow to an assassin, otherwise even his own royal footprints would not be his own.

The only thing Reggie now disliked about Palm Beach was that it was in America. If you killed someone, it wasn't like Zaire, where things could be arranged properly among civilized men. In America, they reacted toward killing like hysterics. They would lock you up and he couldn't afford time in jail for an American kill. But once you had the blood of men on your hands, elephants, deer and goats would never do again. He would have to be careful about his newfound pleasure until after he finished the Korean, if it was the right Korean.

He thought about this while looking at Drake, the butler. He wondered what Drake's heart would look like pumping pitifully outside the chest cavity.

"What do you want me to do with your dinner knife, Master Reggie?" asked the butler, seeing it pointed in his direction.

"Nothing," sighed Reggie. Palm Beach was in America.

He went back to the photograph of the stone. The pattern was clear now after so many centuries. Sword, fire, traps, one thing after another. Reginald Woburn III imagined how Prince Wo's followers must have been discouraged as each method appeared to fail. But they hadn't failed really. There were just six ways that showed what wouldn't work.

The seventh would.

Chapter Four

It was one of those painfully beautiful Bahamian mornings on Little Exuma, the first sun kiss of the horizon in purples and blues and reds like some lucky watercolor accident by a child with the sky for a canvas.

Herons perched on mangrove roots and the bonefish darted from flats to swamp just a little bit more safely that morning, because Bonefish Charlie was dead, and the first thing the constable said was not to let the tourists know.

Bonefish Charlie, who had guided so many tourists around the shallows of Little Exuma to catch the jet-fast game fish with the sharp teeth and fighting heart, let the water wash his eyes and did not blink, let the water wash his nose and made no bubbles, let the water clean his mouth and small fish swim around his teeth.

Bonefish Charlie had been maneuvered into the

twisted mangrove roots in such a way that for a
short while that night, as the tide rose, he could
breathe. And then, as the tide rose just a bit more,
he could only breathe water. Bonefish Charlie,
who the natives had always said was more bonefish than man, wasn't. The proof positive was
wedged into the roots as the tide went out. Bonefish thrived under the mangrove roots when the
tide came in and Bonefish Charlie hadn't.

"It ain't a morder," said the constable in that
strange chopped British accent of the Bahamas,
part British, part African, part Carib Indian, and
part anyone else who traded and pirated in these
waters over the centuries. "Not a morder and
don't you be tellin' de white people."

"I tell not a soul. May my tongue cleave to the
roof of me mouth until it touch bone," said Basket
Mary, who wove and sold baskets to the tourists
down by Government House.

"Just don' tell de whites," said the constable.
Whites meant tourists, and anything smacking of
murder was bad for the tourist business. But the
constable was her cousin and he knew that it was
too much of a horrible incident for Basket Mary to
keep to herself. She would, of course, tell it to
friends until she died. She would tell how she had
found Bonefish Charlie and what he looked like
with "the fishes who was always his friends
swimmin' in his mouth like they found a coral in
his teeth."

And then with a great understanding laugh she would add that it probably was the first time his teeth were ever clean.

All people died sooner or later and better to laugh in the Bahamian sun than to go around like whites on the grim business of changing a world that never really changed anyway. There would be other bonefishermen and other sunrises and other men to love other women and Bonefish Charlie was a good man so that was that. But, for the morning, it was a grievous and dangerous thing to talk about among the natives, wondering who had killed Bonefish Charlie because the last place in the world he would have drowned accidentally would have been in the mangrove roots he knew so well.

It instantly replaced the news that there was a new owner of the Del Ray Promotions, owners of the new condominiums being put up for white folks. Strange fellows. Seemed to know the island a bit. Some of the friends of Basket Mary said there had been a family here like them with that name some time ago, but they had left to go to England and other places. Stuck together, they did, and some said they were here when the slaves were brought in, but of course it was not nearly so interesting a subject as the death of Bonefish Charlie in his mangrove swamp.

Reginald Woburn III met the apologetic constable at his office and heard with horror that his bonefishing guide would not be able to take him out again that day.

"Bad heart, Mr. Woburn, sir," said the constable. "But we got others just as good. You bought a good place here and we are glad you are here. We are a friendly island. We got the friendly beaches. We got the sun."

"Thank you," said Reggie. Fellow sounded so much like an advertisement, he thought. He waited until the constable was gone and then retired into a room without windows. He flicked on a harsh single-beam light set in the ceiling. It illuminated a great round stone resting on a green velvet table. He shut the door behind him and locked it securely, then approached the table and fell to his knees where he lovingly gave one strong kiss to the carved stone from a kingdom where his ancestors had ruled.

Somehow the message was even clearer when he read it from the stone itself. His time had come. He was the first son of the first son of the direct line of his family. If the seventh stone were correct, the Korean's head would go like a ripe plum from a thin vine.

Of course, there were still some mysteries about the stone. He pondered one strange word. It translated roughly as one house, two heads of one master. Two plums on the vine. Was that poetic? Or was the stone more knowing, more accurate than he even dared hope? He looked now on the words for how he would kill and he saw they could also be translated as "need to kill." The stone knew. It knew about him.

He had needed the bonefish guide the evening before more than he had ever needed a woman, or needed water when he was thirsty. The man he had wrestled into the roots looked on helplessly as the water rose. Even now the man's words gave him a delicious little thrill.

"Why you laughin', mon?" Bonefish Charlie had asked.

He was laughing, of course, because it was such a delicious satisfaction, a little appetizer before the plums. Plums. That was what the stone said. Did that mean he would have to kill more than one Korean? If so, who was the other one?

He had already hired the best eavesdropping specialist to implant all the latest devices in the Korean's condo. This too had been written in the stone, thousands of years before these devices were invented. What else could be the meaning of "ears better than ears, eyes better than eyes will be in your power at the beginning of the kill?" They had known that his would be the age for revenge. Reggie would know the every spoken word of the Korean and the white man who was with him. Might plums mean two Koreans or a white and a Korean?

Outside, someone was knocking at the door and

he ignored it. He wanted to think about the meaning of the stone's message.

Remo had a wonderful way to detect when he was being ignored. No one was answering. No one answered when he picked up the phone and pushed all the extension buttons. No one answered when he hit the courtesy buzzer that promised instant service. The sign had said: "We're here before your finger leaves the buzzer."

His finger had left the buzzer, then buzzed again. The comfort coordinator wasn't there, the headwaiter wasn't there, the assistant headwaiter wasn't there, maintenance wasn't there, nor was someone called the "fun facilitator."

So Remo used a little trick that always seemed to work for room service and should work at the "full-service condominium—the only way it's not a first-class hotel is that you own it."

He took out part of a wall and hurled a desk through it. The desk landed on a grove of aloe plants in bloom. Papers once securely filed in the desk now fluttered down to the beach. Then he took out a window. It was already loose. Most of the wall surrounding it was already in the aloe bed outside.

Three people in white with red sashes around their waists came running.

"Good. Are you room service?" Remo asked.

The three looked nervously at the inside of the office, unobstructed now by a wall or a window.

It was a wonderful view. They didn't see any tools he had used to take it out. He must have done it with his hands, they realized, and in unison, all said: "You rang, sir?"

"Right," said Remo. "I would like some fresh water and some rice."

"We have the Del Ray Bahamas Breakfast which consists of corn muffins, bacon, eggs and toast, with sweet rolls to taste."

"I want fresh water and I want rice," Remo said.

"We can make you rice."

"No, you can't make me rice. You can't make rice. You don't know how to make rice."

"Our rice is delicate, each grain a separate morsel."

"Right," Remo said. "You don't know how to make rice. You've got to be able to clump it. That's how you make rice. Good and clumpy."

They all glanced at the missing wall. They wondered what the new owner would say about the wall, but they *knew* what they would say about the rice.

"Clumpy is right."

"Like delicious mush," said the headwaiter.

"Right," said Remo. He followed them into the main kitchen, past burning pig meat and rancid sugared rolls, their poisonous sugared raisins rotting in the morning heat. He made sure he got a sealed bag of rice because an open one might pick up the stench. In his days before training, he had longed for a strip of bacon and had been told that someday he would consider it as unpleasant as any other dead body of any other animal.

Now he couldn't remember how he had ever liked it.

He got the rice and said thank you. One of the cooks wanted to prepare it but was told Remo liked it sticky.

"He like it that way?"

"Nobody's asking you to eat it," Remo said to the cook, and to the waiter smiling for instructions, he said, "Get out of the way."

Someone had planted a palm tree the day before that was supposed to give shade to the entrance to his and Chiun's condo. Remo didn't like it there so he crushed its trunk. He didn't like the concrete stairs either so he turned the bottom one to sand and gravel to see how it would look. Inside, Chiun was making brush strokes on a historic parchment for Sinanju.

"Did Smith call?" Remo asked.

"Not today, not yesterday, not the day before."

"Okay," said Remo.

"Isn't this vacation fun?" Chiun said. "There is so much of history I must catch up on."

"You like it," Remo said. "I'm making the rice."

"This is your vacation," Chiun said. "Let them make the rice." He made the brush strokes for Sinanju. The brush itself seemed to make these sacred marks. For several years of the history he was writing, he did not mention that the new master he was training was white. Now he faced the problem of putting that fact into the history without making it look as if he had intentionally withheld it earlier.

He had once toyed with the idea of just never mentioning that Chiun, hopefully one day to be called the Great Chiun, would have passed on the secrets of Sinanju to a white. Nowhere else was the race of each Master of Sinanju mentioned. Was it mentioned that the Great Wang was Oriental? Or that he was Korean or from Sinanju? And what of Pak or We or Deyu? Was it mentioned that these Masters were all from Sinanju in Korea?

Therefore, would Chiun be to blame for not mentioning that Remo was not from the Orient or Korea or Sinanju? Chiun asked himself this question forthrightly. Unfortunately, he was interrupted before he had a chance to tell himself forthrightly that he could not be blamed for anything.

"Little Father," said Remo. "I am angry and I don't know what I am angry about. I knock down walls for no reason. I want to do something but I don't know what I want to do. I feel I am losing something."

Chiun thought silently for a moment.

"Little Father, I'm going insane. I'm losing myself."

Chiun nodded slowly. The answer was clear.

While he would understand it as natural for him and blameless of him not to mention that Remo was white, what would Remo do when he wrote the history of *his* Masterhood? Would Remo tell that he was white, thus indicating that for years, the Great Chiun had lied? Would Chiun then cease to be the Great Chiun? These things had to be considered.

"So what do you say?" asked Remo.

"About what," said Chiun.

"Am I going crazy?"

"No," said Chiun. "I trained you."

Chiun pressed in a few more brush strokes. Perhaps there might be hints of Remo's whiteness, then a feeling of how Remo became Sinanju and then Korean and, of course, from the village. It could appear that Chiun had found under that ugly white exterior a true Korean, proud and noble.

It could appear that way, but would Remo let it be? He knew Remo. He never felt any shame in his being white. He would never hide it.

"Chiun, I feel strange almost all the time, as if things are out of order in me. Is it my training? Did you ever go through this?"

Chiun put down the brush. "Everything is a cycle. Some things happen so quickly that people do not see them, and others happen so *slowly* that people do not see them. But when you are Sinanju, you are aware of cycles. You are aware that slow and fast are both invisible. You are aware of anger in yourself that others, in their sloth and their meat-eating and their crude breathing, do not see."

"I took out a wall because I couldn't get room service fast enough, Little Father."

"Did you get it?"

"Yes," Remo said.

"Then you are the first person in the Caribbean ever to get something when he wanted it."

Chiun added to the parchment another sign for great teaching. He had many of them in his history.

"I want to do something, anything. This rest is making everything worse," Remo said. He looked out onto the beach. Pure white, stretching miles. Turquoise-blue water. White-bellied gulls with dip and pivot, moving on the sun breezes of the morning. "This place is driving me crazy."

"If you need something, we will study the histories," Chiun said.

"I studied them," said Remo, reeling off the facts of the lineage of the House of Sinanju, starting with the first who had to feed the village and moving on through the centuries to the feats of the Great Wang, the lesser Wang, what each had learned and each had taught and what someday Remo would teach.

"You've never learned tributes," Chiun said. "The very lifeblood of the village of Sinanju has never been learned."

"I don't want to learn tributes, Little Father.

I'm not in this for the money. I'm an American. I love my country."

"Eeeeeyah," wailed Chiun, a delicate hand clutching his breast. "Words that stab this bosom. Lo, that I should still hear such ignorance. Where, O great Masters before me, have I gone wrong? That after all these years, a professional assassin should still utter such words?"

"You always knew that," Remo said. "I never cared about the money. If Sinanju needed the money, I would supply it. But you've still got gold statues from Alexander the Great in that mudhole in Korea and they're never going to starve. So we don't have to kill for some make-believe-poor villagers to live."

"Betrayal," said Chiun.

"Nothing new," Remo said. He looked out at that stinking white beach again. He and Chiun had been here for days. Maybe three of them.

"I've got to do something," said Remo. He wondered if he could break a beach. But a beach was already broken. Broken rock or coral in small parts. He wondered if he could put a beach back together again, since it was broken to start with.

"Then let us learn tribute. Or, as an American merchant might say, billing and accounts receivable."

"I am so jumpy, even that. Okay. Let's go through tribute. You don't have to use English. You taught me Korean."

"True, but I am beginning to mention in my

histories that sometimes the language of English was used in my training of you."

"Only now? Why now, when now I'm learning only in Korean and at first I learned only in English?"

"Get the scroll," said Chiun.

The scroll was in one of the fourteen steamer trunks Chiun always had moved from residence to residence. Only two were needed for his clothing and the rest carried mostly bric-a-brac but also many of Sinanju's scrolls. Chiun had tried putting the scrolls on a computer once but the computer had erased a page with his name on it and Chiun had erased the computer salesman.

Remo found the first scroll of tribute which included geese and goslings, barley and millet and a copper statue of a god now dead.

By the time they were into Cathay kings and gold bullion, Remo's mind was wandering. When they got to a point that Chiun said was the most important of all so far, Remo got up to cook the rice.

"Sit. This is most important." And Chiun told about a prince who was willing to pay, but not publicly.

"Is that the last?" Remo said.

"For today, yes," Chiun said.

"Okay. Go ahead," said Remo. He wondered if gulls thought. And if they thought, what did they think? Did sand think? Was the rice really fresh? Should he wear sandals that day? All these things he thought while Chiun explained that it must never be thought that an assassin was not paid, because then others would try not to pay. This had happened once and it was why this one prince had to be chased throughout the known world.

"One defense after another, until six of his defenses were shown to be useless; from one land to another, thus showing Rome and China and Crete and the Scythians that Sinanju was not to be dishonored."

"So where was he killed?" asked Remo.

"He didn't have to be killed. The purpose was to defend the sacred immutable truth that an assassin must be paid. While you, you don't even care about tributes and then you complain to me that you are going crazy."

"What happened to that prince who didn't pay?" Remo asked again.

"He was shorn of kingdom and safe place to sleep, shorn of glory and honor, sent like a thief into the night, cringing like the lowest vermin."

"Did we miss?" Remo asked. "Did Sinanju miss?"

"Make the rice," said Chiun.

"We missed, didn't we?" asked Remo, his face suddenly sparkling.

"Now, you listen. With happiness on your face. If you could see your evil white grin, such shame you would feel."

"I don't feel shame. I want to hear how the

prince was finished. Show me his head. That was a popular one in Baghdad, hanging the head on a wall. I want to see that one."

"He was humiliated," Chiun said.

"We didn't get him, did we? What's this about only one world to hide in and we are in the same world so there is never a place to hide. No one can hide. Even we can't hide. Where did he hide, Little Father?"

"The rice."

"I am enjoying my vacation now," said Remo. "I want to know where he hid. Athens? Rome? Cathay?"

"This," said Chiun, "is not a good vacation."

"Was it the Great Wang who missed or who?"

"Now, you listen," said Chiun and folded his robe and put the scroll away inside it. There was a reason Remo had never wanted to study tributes to Sinanju. It was obvious. He wasn't ready for it and Chiun was not going to try to transform a pale piece of a pig's ear into a real Master of Sinanju. Some things were beyond even the Great Chiun.

Warner Dabney hated two things. The first was failure and the second was admitting it, and now the two things he hated most he had to endure with a client who had more money than a gang of Arabs.

He saw his commission go down the drain in the handful of bugging devices, some still covered with plaster, that were in his briefcase as he tried to explain to Mr. Woburn why the pair could not be bugged.

Mr. Woburn had the coldest eyes that Dabney had ever seen in a human skull. His movements were strange, strange even for a really rich kid used to being waited on. Slow. Slow hands and face like stone. And because this rich Woburn kid wasn't talking, wasn't saying anything, like some damned king on some damned throne, Warner Dabney of Dabney Security Systems Inc. had to say more than he wanted.

He went through descriptions of bug implants in the wall, beam riders that could hear on a focused beam, and what he finally had to tell Mr. Woburn was:

"I failed. I friggin' failed, Mr. Woburn, and I'm sorry."

"You say there is nothing you picked up from any of their conversations?"

"Not exactly nothing. We got a word."

"What's the word?"

"Rice . . . nothing else. It mean something?"

"It means that Koreans frequently eat rice," Reginald Woburn III said.

"I mean these guys picked up everything. Everything. Like it was spring housecleaning. You know. Like you and I could go into a room and see a cigarette in an ashtray and like pick it up, you know. They went into their place and like it was cleaning up, they got rid of all the bugs. I was outside during some of it and they didn't even discuss it. Here I am with my beam listeners and computer chips and I'm using my own ears to eavesdrop and these guys, it's the weirdest thing. They're not talking about the bugs, they're just unpacking, and out go the bugs with an empty box of Kleenex."

"You will be paid in full," said Reggie.

"Sir?"

"Thank you. You may leave."

"But you know I didn't get one sentence of what they said, Mr. Woburn."

"We pay our bills for services rendered. We are reliable. We are paying you. You are excused," said Reggie.

Wonderful, Reggie thought. Technology had failed because technology was only of one age. He knew now he was of the ages and that was why he used the ears that could hear beyond hearing, as the stone had said. Some little spy somewhere could not. Why was the man still standing there in his office with his mouth open?

"Is there anything else I can do for you, Mr. Woburn?"

Hadn't he told him already he was excused?

"Warner Dabney is here for your service. These guys were real, extra special tough. But the next time . . ." Dabney said.

"What is your name again?" He would have to be shown that when he was excused, it meant excused.

"Dabney, sir. Warner Dabney."

"Warner, give me your hand," said Reggie. He reached into the desk. There was a pin inside the desk with a chemical to suppress the heartbeat. It had been created for surgery by one of Woburn's pharmaceutical firms, but it had yet to be tested on humans. The problem was diluting the powerful formula to make it safe. One part per million could kill.

Warner Dabney hesitantly put forward his hand. When a rich client who paid even for failures asked for something silly, you didn't say no. Warner had never been paid for a failure before.

"Thank you," said Reginald, taking the upraised palm and very gently stroking the pads of the man's fingertips. Then Reggie smiled and put the pin into the palm. Warner Dabney dropped like a stone. Bang. He was on the floor. Reginald put back the needle. The product had been tested on humans. It worked.

The constabulary agreed on the telephone that the death was obviously a heart attack and that Del Ray Promotions could just go ahead and plant him.

"His head still on his body?"

"Yes, officer," said Reggie.

"Den dat death be natural. In the Caribbean, we are most careful about investigating unnatural deaths. If that mon be dead with an arrow in his heart, no way we say that be a natural death, sir."

"I agree with you, constable, and please convey our appreciation to Government House and your fine island people for this warm and most hospitable welcome we have received from you this day."

"As you wish, your Highness," said the constable, suddenly wondering why he had said that. And then he remembered. He had the same feeling speaking to Mr. Woburn that he did when he stood at parade rest before Queen Elizabeth of Great Britain. He apologized to Mr. Woburn for the slip of tongue.

"We accept your apology," said Reggie.

As Warner Dabney was leaving the office, heels first in the hands of two porters, Reginald Woburn III could not suppress the true exhilaration at having the first thrust at his enemies succeed.

It was not his purpose to inform servants of his thinking. Warner Dabney had succeeded but had not even known he had succeeded. But seeing that these two routinely handled eavesdropping devices, he had discovered that the two had been exposed to this sort of thing before, undoubtedly often. It fit with the picture in Reggie's mind of a professional assassin. They would be used to that kind of things. And when one of the maintenance men explained that one of the condo share owners was the one who had ripped out a wall and said, "Would you believe he did it with his bare hands, sir?" Reginald answered, simply, "We do."

He had found them, or more correctly, they had found him. Now to continue with the way of the seventh stone. Everything was working perfectly.

"Do you wish to charge them for the broken wall, Mr. Woburn?"

"No. We'll just speak to them."

That afternoon, Chiun met the first really respectful white, an owner of the general property, who commiserated with him over ungrateful sons . . . not that Chiun was complaining . . . and about the difficulty in working for a government.

Not that Chiun was complaining about that either. He didn't complain. Even if said government, like all typically white things, did not appreciate his work. How white. How American.

"You did say American, didn't you?" said Reggie happily, and he got a nod.

"I thought we heard you," he said.

The next day, Remo had a phone call from Smith that there was urgent government business and when Remo left by car, Reginald Woburn III did a little joyous dance in what was left of the aloe bed.

It was working.

Chapter Five

Smith was waiting at the airport with a valise and a wallet. His gaunt face was twisted with strain.

"I'm sorry. I know you need a vacation desperately, but I had to put you on again," he said, and said nothing more until they reached his car, a gray Chevrolet compact. This man had millions at his disposal, Remo knew, and could fly about in his own jet if he wished. Yet he traveled economy class, used the least expensive car he could, and never wasted a penny even though no government oversight committee would ever get a chance to look at the organization's expenditures. They had chosen the right man when they had chosen Smith, thought Remo.

He glanced at the wallet. It contained a press pass to the White House. Inside the valise were a white shirt, a suit the color of a nasal decongestant and a tie to match.

"I take it the suit's for me," Remo said as the car left the parking lot.

"Yes. You can't enter the White House press corps without it."

"Why the color of medicine? Who would wear a suit this color?"

"You've got to look like a reporter," Smith said.

Remo looked at the suit again. A pinkish gray. It was really a pinkish gray.

"Do they get special prices on these clothes?" he asked.

"No. They like it. They choose colors like that. Not the television reporters. They're mostly actors and actresses and they know how to dress. Real reporters dress like that and you're going to be one. And I'm sorry I'm interrupting your vacation."

"I was going crazy doing nothing," Remo said.

"Be careful," Smith said. "I mean it. Watch yourself."

Remo reached over to the steering wheel, and putting the pads of his thumb and index finger around the plastic, caught the very movement of the material itself. Even before the world had known of atoms and molecules, Sinanju had known that everything was movement of particles that attracted and repelled.

Sinanju knew that nothing was still; everything was movement. Remo felt the movement of the car and breathed in air more stale because of the

closed windows. He could feel the warm smooth-
ness of the gray plastic wheel and then the slight
indentations and pits where the plastic had dried
uneven, although it looked smooth to the eye.
Through his fingers, he sensed the mass of the
wheel, the sticky plasticness of it, the strain of the
materials and then the movement of the cosmos
on that scale too small for the eye to see, just as the
universe was too large to see. In an instant, it was
one and then he guided just one atom in one mole-
cule into another orbit by the most minute
charge, a thought transmitted through a finger-
tip, and the steering wheel had a three-quarter-
inch gap in it where his fingers had touched.

To Smith, it looked as if Remo had reached
over and made a section of the wheel disappear. It
happened that quickly. He was sure Remo had
broken it off somehow and hidden it somewhere.
Magic.

"So I need a rest. So I'm not up to my level.
Who's going to be a danger to me?" asked Remo.
"Who is a problem? I can take whoever we need
in my sleep. Where is the problem?"

"I guess for your continued health. Growth. I
don't know. But I do know if we weren't desperate, I never would have gotten you back from
your vacation."

"I had a vacation. I've been down at that island
forever. It must be going on, my God, four days,"
Remo said.

"The President is going to be killed this afternoon at his news conference."

"Who told you?" Remo asked.

"The killer."

"You mean it's a threat?"

"No," Smith said. "Threats are just words. I wouldn't have called you up here for a threat. The President of the United States gets a hundred threats a week and the Secret Service investigates and puts the name in the file. If we didn't have it all on computers, we'd have to have a warehouse for the names."

"How do you know he'll succeed, this killer?" Remo asked.

"Because he's already had success," said Smith. He slipped a note out of his coat pocket and without taking his eyes off the road slipped it to Remo. It read:

"Not now, but Thursday at two P.M."

"So?" said Remo. "What's that all about?"

"The note came wrapped around a little bomb the President found in his suit pocket. Now he was having lunch with an important fund-raiser in his election. A little private lunch with a Mr. Abner Wooster. He heard a ringing in his suit. He felt a bulge and then found the bomb. No larger than a little calculator but it had enough explosive to make him into coleslaw. The businessman was immediately ushered out by the Secret Service."

"Okay, so he's your suspect."

"Not so easy," Smith said. "That night, the President was brushing his teeth and he heard a ringing sound. This time inside his bathrobe." Smith again reached into his pocket and peeled off another note, same size, same lettering, same message.

"So they got his valet, Robert Cawon, out of there. It didn't work." He peeled off yet another note from his pocket. He turned down a large boulevard. Remo just glanced at the note; it was the same as the other two.

"Dale Freewo," said Smith.

"Who was he?"

"The new Secret Service agent assigned to protect the President," said Smith.

"Another bomb?"

"Right. Inside the new vest Freewo had brought him, the armored vest to protect him in case a bomb went off in his suit or bathrobe," Smith said.

"Why do I have to use a cover as a reporter?" Remo asked.

"Because two P.M. Thursday, today, is the President's regularly scheduled new conference. The killer must have known that. You've got to protect him."

"What am I supposed to do if the bombs are already planted on him?" Remo asked.

"I'm not sure, Remo, but in the middle of the night, I saw the President of my country tremble and I just could not tell him that we would not be there, even at the risk of our exposure. They've had the Secret Service, the FBI, even the CIA looking into it and they've gotten nothing. It's you, Remo. Save him if you can. And get the killer."

"You think he's got a chance to succeed, don't you?" Remo asked.

"More than a chance," Smith said and then the car suddenly veered on its mushy American shock absorbers.

"Can you replace the section you took out?" Smith asked.

"I didn't take it out," Remo said.

"What did you do then? I've got a hole in my steering wheel."

"I don't know. I can't explain it. Do I have to wear this suit?"

"It will make you inconspicuous," said Smith, who let him off several blocks from the White House.

The press conference was in the Rose Garden. The President wanted to announce the best third quarter of business in the history of the country. The unemployment rate was down, inflation was down. Production was up. Poor Americans had more real dollars and were happily spending them, making other Americans better off. In fact, incredibly fewer than one-tenth of one percent of the population were in dire straits, an unheard-of broad range of prosperity never before achieved in any civilization.

"Mr. President, what are you doing about the people in dire straits?" That was the first question. The second question was why was the President so callous toward the small minority of one-tenth of one percent. Was it because they were so small and therefore defenseless?

The next question was if he felt that the tenth of a percent did not prove that reliance on free enterprise was too heartless and that major government programs were needed, lest America be revealed to the world as a heartless dictatorship.

Had the President ever been in that one-tenth of one percent?

For twenty minutes, there were nothing but questions about the tenth of a percent doing poorly until the President said he had a plan to eliminate that problem, whereupon the press corps moved to foreign policy. The President mentioned a new peace treaty America helped arrange to stop a thirty-year-old border war in Africa. There were no questions.

Remo watched the President, watched everyone near him. He could sense the President was nervous. He looked at his watch a few times. That brought a question about whether the watch was broken and how had his presidency brought about its breakdown.

Remo glanced at a watch next to him. Two P.M. came and two P.M. went. Nobody moved.

Nothing went off and the President called the press conference over on the last question of did he think the tenth of one percent, the disregarded tenth of one percent, those dire-straits people having fallen through the safety net of human concern, did they come from the same failure of his government as his watch?

"No," said the President with a smile, a little bit happier this moment because it was 2:05 P.M. As he turned, a man with straight black hair and Malaysian dark features ran from behind a camera with a sword, screaming.

"Death to you. Death to you."

The man's movements were so sudden and the Secret Service so stunned by a physical attack from the press section that Remo saw the man would make it to the podium in the Rose Garden with his sword before he could be stopped. From the front row, Remo flipped his cardboard notebook at the man.

It looked merely as though he opened his hand but the notebook sailed out at such velocity that it tore through the sword hand and the man arrived at the podium with a limp wrist, a cry of death on his lips, and thrusting nothing into the President's chest because the sword was tumbling uselessly about the lawn.

The Secret Service wrestled him to the ground, got the President out of the Rose Garden, and then an alarm went off on the man, followed by a pop. The pop was a red gushy thing blowing through the air. It was his heart. Something had blown it out of his chest cavity.

After checking press credentials, the assailant was identified as Du Wok of the Indonesian Press Service. The man previously had been a solid newspaperman, was not open to bribes because he had an independent income and generally there was only mystery as to why he had attacked the President. He had no political affiliations whatsoever, which of course made him quite different from most Indonesians, who were either with the government or in hiding.

That night, at Smith's request, Remo stayed with the President. No more notes were found nor were any bombs found. Remo stayed three days, wearing the medicine-colored suit. On the last day, he even stayed in a far wing of the White House.

And still no notes, no reason why an Indonesian named Du Wok had attempted to kill the President. Even more puzzling was how he got the notes into the President's clothing. The best guess was that there was a network. But why did the network want to assassinate the President?

Remo was on his way back to his vacation when his plane was turned around in flight for some federal emergency. The pilot banked toward Dulles International Airport and the passengers began grumbling. All the passengers were off-loaded except Remo, who was signaled into a small booth.

Smith waited inside the booth. Silently he handed Remo a piece of white paper. It was the same size as those that had wrapped the bombs found on the President.

"Have they gotten into his clothes again?" asked Remo.

"We should be so lucky," said Smith.

"They killed him?"

"We should be so lucky," Smith said. "A President's important but he's not Montana, Minnesota, Iowa and if the winds are wrong, the entire Midwest through to Chicago."

"How are they going to blow up all of middle America? They're not the Russians," Remo said.

"They don't have to be. Besides, some things could be worse than a few atomic bombs," Smith said.

Reginald Woburn III wore shorts, a white T-shirt and sandals, and happily hummed to himself. He was watching a film. There was Du Wok with a sword. There was the notebook. Reggie ran it backward and the notebook went from the sword hand back to the thrower. The film had been taken with an incredibly high-speed camera. If it hadn't, it would not have caught the motion of the man in the pink-gray suit. One of the problems was, there were seven-

teen suits just like it. But this was one of the only
three in the front row. And the film he had was
the only one shot with enough frames per second
to capture the movement of the notebook.
Indeed, the book had been moving so fast it was
shredding because the air acted like sandpaper
against its pages.

Reggie recognized the man. The American.
The second plum. It was all so clear it was almost
easy. First the eavesdropping devices that did not
work. That showed what they did professionally,
because only professionals would be used to being
bugged. If indeed this American was somehow
from the family of the old Korean, they would be
working for only the highest power in the land.
And the old one had mentioned something about
the government when he was talking to Reggie.
So it had been natural: threaten the President and
they would have to come to his aid. When Remo
left the Del Ray condominium suddenly after the
notes to the President, Reggie was sure that he
had found his men. Or more accurately, that they
had come to him, for the great secret of the
seventh stone was that they themselves were going
to show him how to kill them.

Reginald watched the high-speed camera catch
the action again. It was a white wrist and a white
hand. It was indeed the second plum. Reggie had
set the stage and there was the actor. He ran the
film again and calculated the force of the note-

book. And the wrist had hardly moved in throwing it. Phenomenal.

They were the ones he sought, Reginald knew. He had expected them both to be Koreans with Korean features, but he was sure that the white one was somehow related to the old one, and he knew the old one must be just as awesome as the white. He could see how one of these would be able to chase a prince and his army across the world and off the maps of the world. They were frightening. He watched the movement of the wrist again. It was so natural, so economical. He knew others might be impressed with the result, but he was looking at the source. If he had not been searching for this, if he had not known it was there, he never would have seen it in the one true way of seeing anything. Understanding it. But there it was, more frightening and somehow more desirable than even that first bull elephant he had killed.

And the two of them had looked like only human beings at first. Reggie found himself humming an old prayer and then he realized it was in the language his father had taught him for gods long dead in lands not even remembered. The kingdom Prince Wo had ruled was gone. But the power of the Korean was not. It had been worth the wait.

His telephone was ringing. It was his father. The Woks from Djakarta, Indonesia, were complaining to his father that Reggie had killed their blessed son Du and that while they recognized the first son of the first son as the true lord by right, this did not include getting killed.

"Father," said Reginald. "It does."

"How do you expect to keep the line of the family together if you get them killed?"

"We'll take care of that," said Reggie.

"Do you have others with you?"

"No, we don't," said Reginald. "But we will take care of it."

As he hung up the telephone, Reggie thought that while he might have people working for him, he had no one *with* him. Princes never did. They were always alone.

In Djakarta, the family of Wok received a special silver-and-jade platter sent by the first-born of the firstborn in the direct line of Prince Wo.

In the center covered by fine silks was the special surprise. Of such wonder was it, such grandness were the jewels under the silk, that Reginald Woburn III had one request. He wanted the children of the Wok family present for the unveiling of the gift. He was truly repentant for the loss of one of their members serving him and while the gift could never compensate for a life, it most certainly would show his feelings.

It had one warning. They could not remove the silk hastily because it would ruin the fine lacquers and spun gold. It had to be unwrapped under precise instructions and for that they would have to be talked through it on the telephone. Considering that the outside corners each held gems worth over a hundred thousand dollars, the Woks could only imagine what the value of the center would be.

"Are the babies there? I want the babies, no matter how young, to be there," said Reggie. "They must remember this day."

"Yes, everyone."

"Everyone?" Reggie asked.

There was a long pause.

"Why would you not think everyone is here?"

"Because we suspect that Ree Wok is disloyal. We do not wish for him to share in this treasure if he is not there," Reggie said.

"Reginald, you really do have eyes across seas for thousands of miles. The one of whom you speak was reluctant. How did you see that?"

"We will start without him," Reggie said, "because we see greater things. We see into your hearts. Now, is the platter on the floor?"

"Yes."

"There are no tables or chairs there?"

"No."

"Everybody gather round," said Reggie. "Now place the youngest child directly over the silk pile. Is it there?"

"Yes, yes. My arms are getting tired holding him."

"Just put him down."

"Feetfirst?"

"Any way," said Reggie. Suddenly there was a clicking on the line and all he could hear was transoceanic interference, a crackling and then the line was dead.

"Hello," he said and no one answered.

Within the hour, Ree Wok, the man who was not at the family gathering, telephoned.

"Thank you," he said. "Thank you for saving me."

"Did any escape?" Reggie asked.

"None. The entire house collapsed. Pieces were found a half-mile away, I have heard."

"Ree Wok, we declare you now head of the Wok clan."

"Yes, great Prince. But there are no Woks left."

"Take a wife," said Reggie. "We command it."

"Yes, great Prince."

Father was on the phone shortly thereafter and Reggie had to explain that he had reasons for what he did and the family had grown quite sloppy over the centuries and that finally the family would return to its full glory with the Koreans gone.

"Father," he concluded. "We just don't have time for you."

"Are they gone yet, the Koreans?"

"You don't even know who they are," said Reggie to the silly old man.

"Have you killed them?"

"We will," Reggie said.

(History of Sinanju from the gracious pen of Chiun, for those to come, that the House of Sinanju shall in its glory prosper and survive.)

"And through the years, Chiun would accept no obstacle, even though the pupil was not from precisely what was considered the old borders of the village. As has been mentioned in the histories, these borders changed often. Sometimes those who lived west of the mill were considered Sinanju. Sometimes not. Who was to say where the borders in one age began and where in another they left off? As has been mentioned in previous histories by Chiun, there might be those who would question, not without some foundation, whether Chiun's pupil was indeed born within the formal boundaries of the village. There are always those who will quibble.

"Nevertheless, through the years, Remo showed that Chiun could raise him to that level which could not be denied. He was Sinanju, even if he had been born as far away as the south village. Nay, even Peking or Tokyo, which he was not.

"During the time of rest, Chiun took Remo to an island in the new world Chiun had discovered. (See: Discovery of America, Emperor Who Would Not Serve.)

"And it came to pass that a total stranger came

into Chiun and mentioning that Remo had been gone many days now bordering on weeks, said, 'Where has your son gone?'

" 'Son,' answered Chiun. 'Why do you say that?'

" 'Because,' said this simple but wise stranger, 'there is something about him that is so much your son. Or even your brother.'

"Here, from the lips of a third person, was proof that Remo, the pupil, was definitely of Sinanju even if he had been born, in the eyes of some, far west of the old mill."

"Yes, Mr. President," said Smith into the special device that would allow his voice to be scrambled. Only a telephone in the White House could unscramble it.

"He has been there for a week, sir," Smith said.

"Then why hasn't he stopped it?" the President said.

"I don't know, sir."

"Should I leave Washington?"

"I don't know."

"Well, dammit, Smith, what do you know? You run the organization that's supposed to know everything. What do you know?"

"He's on it, sir. And I don't know his methods. Only one other person does."

"The old Oriental? I like him. Use him too."

"I am afraid, sir, that according to the protocols under which I operate, you cannot

order me to do things. You can only suggest or
order me to disband. This was to protect the
country from my organization in case a President
should try to misuse it."

"I don't see how trying to save twenty million
people from dying a horrible death is misusing
your organization."

Smith knew that the death threats and that
crazed Indonesian newsman trying to kill him
with a sword had gotten to the President. He was
not about to tell this distraught leader that the
Oriental whom the President liked so much
because he was old too had become difficult
because Smith was using Remo when Remo
should have been resting.

Smith was only glad that Remo demonstrated
that even while he was at less than peak, he was
still far beyond anything else in the field he might
come up against.

So Smith assured the President that the
Oriental was not needed.

"I will call you again only if it is absolutely
necessary, sir. I don't think for the sake of our
ongoing cover, we should be talking this much,"
Smith said.

"All right," said the President.

But before the day was out, Smith was phoning
him. He had seen projected weather reports about
a change in the jet stream and the President was
going to have to leave Washington. The whole
east coast would be in danger too.

Chapter Six

It was Indian country but the danger wasn't the Indians. They were the victims. The rolling hills where antelope and buffalo had grazed until the introduction of the rifle and cash for their skins, actually covered in their scenic beauty a bureaucratic foul-up so dangerous that every department had kept passing it to another department since the First World War.

Underneath grass, far beneath where gophers made their underground villages, were four square miles of nerve gas, the first containers put there in case Kaiser Bill didn't learn his lesson and America needed to use gas warfare in the trenches of France. But at the end of the Great War, later to be given number one, gas warfare was outlawed.

Like all the other countries with standing armies, America kept the gas just in case anyone else would violate the treaty. And then World War II broke out and new, more virulent gas was manufactured in case anyone broke the treaty in that war.

And then the cold war started and one never knew what Russia might do, so more new gas was manufactured.

And there was never a war in which America used gas, nor did any other country, no matter how base its philosophy, until in the Middle East an Arab country based on the principles of "compassion and justice" used it against a fellow Islamic country, based on "justice and compassion."

Like all the other civilized countries who had never used their gas in war, America had been making it since Woodrow Wilson and the Sopwith Camel airplane and had an awful lot of deadly gas. Acres of it. Miles of it.

In the early 1900s, they started stockpiling it with a friendly tribe of Indians in the Pakeeta reservation. The deal was one bottle of whiskey for one can of gas. The can would be buried underground and the Pakeeta would never even have to see it, much less smell it. The Pakeeta had the word of the United States government, a sacred promise from its leader and people. The gas was safe.

Since the Pakeeta chief had already sampled an awful lot of the whiskey the government would give just to store the gas on the Pakeeta reservation just south of Billings, Montana, he took the sacred word of the white man.

International relations being what they were, the entire Pakeeta tribe was able to stay drunk right up until the 1960s, when a new militancy overtook them. They were not going to store the white man's filthy weapons of death for his filthy body-destroying whiskey. They were touching their old roots again and demanded clear water and rich grazing lands and the pure sky of the great spirits. It was not the days of trusting, simple Indians anymore. The U.S. government could keep its whiskey. The Pakeeta wanted their dignity. They wanted cash.

They got the cash and they bought cocaine and whiskey, although the old-timers still liked the old government-issue whiskey better.

They continued to get chemicals in iron drums. One whiff of the sort of deadly gas that had been created could kill a man. A spoonful of the liquid allowed to mist in the air could wipe out a town. A quart would do a state, and the Pakeeta were sitting on four square miles of the drums and the original drums were rusting. Steel did that when buried in water-laden ground.

The steel had been doing that since Kaiser Bill and his Huns. The Department of the Army said it wasn't its problem; the Army had gotten rid of the gas. The Bureau of Indian Affairs wasn't responsible because that was a problem of the land itself and the BIA dealt only with the Indians; it had no jurisdiction under the ground. They kicked it over to the Department of the

Interior, which launched an investigation and blamed the Army.

The drums rusted. Everyone knew they were dangerous. The government formed a high-level committee to investigate and make immediate recommendations. It was 1920 and there was enough gas underground at that time to wipe out Montana. By the time the committee was forming its final subcommittee to finalize its final recommendations, there was enough gas stored under the Pakeeta reservation to wipe out the United States and half the fish in the Atlantic, depending on how strong the winds were. It could also take out part of Canada and if there was a southward flow, settle Central America's problems for a good two centuries.

And then someone, as a little gift, sent a piece of one rusted drum to the Bureau of Indian Affairs, the Department of the Army, the Department of the Interior and to the committee that was still investigating sixty-four years later.

In three mailrooms, every person was killed when the metal touched air coming out of its plastic package. In the fourth mailroom, a vent carried the scent to the second floor, where thirty-two people were left staring dumbly into space, their nervous systems wrecked forever.

The most frightening thing, however, was not the bodies but the note.

"Please check the metal. You will find that it was manufactured by the Rusco Steelworks of

Gary, Indiana, in 1917, precisely for the Army.
And that for one purpose: to store gas. We tried
cleaning off the metal by immersion in chemicals
but as you probably know by now, even the most
severe chemical scrubbing cannot clean this stuff.
We had to remove the metal to get the explosives
into the drums. Quite a chore, considering everything had to be sealed airtight when we did it. But
we're good at placing bombs. Ask the President."

Even before the bodies were cleaned out of the
mailrooms, the second notes arrived, this time
sent to the secretaries of the heads of the depart-
ments, which showed that the sender knew there
would be no one left in the mailrooms to
distribute the letters.

This letter was a puzzle. There was a maze that
someone had to get through in order to get into
the stored drums to dismantle the bomb before it
exploded. There was also a schematic of the bomb
and Army engineers expressed admiration for it.
It could take off approximately fifteen acres of
earth. Given proper jet-stream activity, it could
blow enough poison gas into the air to destroy the
Midwest.

Two men tried to follow the map that came
with the note and were lost. So was a third. It
seemed that not only did the Army Rangers have
to tiptoe through cans of rusting nerve gas, loaded
down with breathing apparatus and suits to keep
their skin safe from air contact, but that there
were people hiding in those underground areas

who knew their way around and who knew how to kill.

And the bomb was going to go off.

Armies were useless. In the underground mazes of drums, ten thousand men were no better than one. In fact, the second note had warned that if more than two men were sent to disarm the bomb, it would be exploded.

One or two special men were needed and after the best of the Rangers were used up on the first day, the President had ordered the Army to step aside. He was going to use other means.

Remo arrived in Billings, Montana, on one of its rare muggy days with a little envelope containing the notes. It was the envelope Smith had given him back at Dulles Airport when the island-bound plane had been diverted back to takeoff. Find the bomb, disarm it and get it out from those rotting drums of poison gas.

"And, Remo," Smith had said, "watch yourself. All right?"

"You want me to do another steering wheel, Smitty?" asked Remo, and then he was off to Billings.

The Pakeeta reservation didn't have teepees but neat houses with pickup trucks, some laundry hanging on the lines of those houses without dryers, and large discount stores. No one was selling blankets and Remo didn't see a feather in anyone's hair. He was asked thirteen times what he was doing there and showed identification from the Bureau of Indian Affairs.

He found the entrance to the gas-storage area, two plain steel doors set into a hill that looked like a bunker. Two guards at the entrance checked his papers.

"Some Army guys go in yesterday, they don't come out on their feet," said one of the guards.

"I'm not Army," Remo said.

"They plenty tough."

"It's not toughness that counts," Remo said with a little smile. "It's sweetness."

"Hey, where's your flashlight?"

"Don't need one."

"You want to leave your money with me?" the guard asked.

"Why?"

"You ain't coming out again and I can use it," the guard said.

"I'm coming out," Remo said.

Inside, he let the darkness fill him. The normal response of a person to dark was anxiety, which strained the nervous system. Fear made the dark darker. In dim light, Remo could adjust his eyes so that he could see normally. But in total darkness, he did a different kind of seeing. It wasn't normal vision with colors and outlines; it was more of a knowing.

The drums were stacked neatly, stretched out in square formations. Remo stayed still and heard a small scurrying sound, probably a hundred yards away. Good, he thought. No gas is escaping because the mice are alive. Of course, some of this gas manufactured in the fifties could attack through the skin. There was World War I and II gas, Korean gas, cold-war gas, Vietnam gas. Better dying through chemistry.

There was moisture here under the earth and there was a certain heaviness in the darkness. Remo tasted the air as he breathed. It was rich as it always was underground.

He moved between the drums according to the map and got lost. The map was useless. But the areas of drums did have borders and they were not that vast, so Remo began cutting the place up in squares, examining each square with eyes and hands, feeling for anything that might be a bomb, anything to indicate that he had reached that drum with sections sawn out, the sections that had killed the people in the government mail-rooms.

It was slow. He stayed there two days. Four times the doors opened showing painfully white light, and voices called out asking Remo if he was all right.

"Yeah, I'm okay. Shut the door."

The Bureau of Indian Affairs said he didn't have to be there. "It's Army responsibility."

"Shut the door," Remo said. He had once been a soldier himself, long ago before his training, and he thought of the dependence on tools that most men had. Man first used a club, then a sharpened stone, and now he was using lasers from space. And every tool man used made him use his own abilities less, so that now most of his senses and muscles were as useless as his appendix. Using what you had: that was the secret of Sinanju.

He found where the Rangers had died. He could feel in the earth where heels had dug in, that desperate strong throb of muscles fighting for life, suddenly having to be used when they had never been used before.

And then suddenly the air was delicate again, not heavy. Another passageway had been opened. Remo was still. He heard them breathing; he heard their fingers work their way along barrels, fingers that were sure of where they were going.

They knew this place underground, for people did not move that quickly in the dark without having been there before. Then they stopped. They were waiting for him, waiting for him to make a sound.

In the dark, the Rangers had been at an awesome disadvantage against these men who knew their way. Remo heard them whisper.

"I don't hear him."

"Shhhhh."

"He still here?"

"Here? How's he gonna get out?"

"So why don't he make no sound?"

"Maybe he's sleeping."

And so, very clearly, Remo said: "Not sleeping, sweetheart. Come and get me."

He heard them move along the ground. They were quieter than most men. Indians probably. Indians could move well, even though most of them were too heavy. Remo moved himself with their rhythms so that they could not possibly hear him. He moved behind one and ever so gently pushed the third rib up into the aorta. Hearts did not pump efficiently with bone jamming into them. Remo put down the first one with smooth quiet in that dark chamber.

Then he followed the other. The other stopped every few steps and listened for his victim. Remo stopped with him.

Finally, Remo whispered, "Guess who?" The Indian stalking in the dark suddenly screamed and tried to run for the exit. But he was caught by the neck and pressed into the ground.

"Hi. I am the great white spirit, come to break your skull," said Remo. "But I will make you a promise. Tell me who paid you, tell me who told you to do these things and I will let you live forever in a land where the water flows free and the skies are pure."

"Hey, man, we just needed the dough. Coke costs. We don't know who is behind it. We just got told there would be Army people coming in and we should kill them and then there would be a guy here and we should get him if we could."

"Who told you?"

"Crazy guy. Said that we would get paid ten grand to kill you and a hundred grand to describe exactly how we did it."

"What did he look like?" Remo asked.

"I don't know. We got an overnight delivery of cash with a phone number. We kind of advertise as guides to this place. Well, we had this phone conversation and he told us the Rangers or somebody was going to come and told us to be ready for them, and hell, when you get seventy-five hundred through Easy Express in the mail, you do tend to give a man service."

"You must remember more," Remo said.

"That's it. You know, we're Indian guides to the public. We don't ask too many questions. We usually get paid in tens and twenties and if we're lucky we can sell a frigging blanket. This man was talking big money."

"Okay. Thank you for your help. I think you've spoken truly," Remo said.

"Let me go then. I told you everything."

"No, I'm going to kill you," Remo said. "This is Indian country and it's a white tradition not to keep our word."

"But you said your word would be good as long as the water flowed."

"Yup," said Remo, severing nerves in the brain with a sharp painless pinch. "That's an old standby. We've used that a lot."

Remo continued his search for the bomb and finally found what he was looking for in the fourteenth quadrant. But it wasn't a bomb. His hands found a smooth plastic coating covering several barrels. It was a sticky substance, thick as a baseball glove, and that was good because no air could escape from that. In fact, any puncture in a barrel would be sealed by this covering. The people knew what they were doing. He found the barrels with the missing sections. The covering just flowed around the sections, keeping the liquefied gas secure inside. In fact, these barrels were not the most dangerous, as Smith had warned him. They were the safest, because they would not leak poison by accident.

But there was no bomb inside. He should have asked the Indians. Why not before he killed them? The problem with killing someone was you always had to get everything you needed first. You never had a second chance.

When Remo came out into the daylight, he had to keep his eyes shut because the sun felt like flamethrowers on his pupils. He heard chanting some distance away. It sounded like a protest.

"No, no, no to death. No, no, no more chemicals. No, no, no to the USA. USA, go away. USA go away."

Remo heard the outside guard move near him.

"Are those Indians?" Remo said.

"No, they come from Carmel, California. They're here to tell the government to stop pushing around the Indians."

"Any Indians there?"

"They don't tell us. They don't let us near them."

When Remo's eyes lost their night sensitivity, he saw television cameras focusing on a line of men and women, some dressed quite fashionably.

"USA, go away. USA, go away."

Behind them was parked a ring of cars like a circle of covered wagons. The sky was just a kiss of blue with cotton-white clouds and the air was light. It felt good to be above ground. Perhaps that was why Remo thought the woman speaking to the television reporter looked so beautiful. She also looked familiar.

He wondered whether he should warn people to evacuate. But evacuate for what? There was no bomb there. Why should anyone go to so much trouble to threaten the government with a bomb that wasn't there? Had he missed the bomb?

He doubted it.

And who would kill two Army Rangers for a bomb that wasn't there? And why wasn't there a demand for something? Free all prisoners or give them ten million dollars or something.

Barrels meticulously cut apart under air-retardant plastic gel, sent to the right people to get a response, those responding getting killed, and then no one touching him and no bomb there. What was it all about? Had they done what they set out to do? If so, what was it?

The woman was a stunner. Rich black hair,

sea-blue eyes and a body that could make a Trappist monk buy a hairpiece.

She was talking about chemicals. She was talking about death. She represented MAC, Mothers and Actresses Against Chemicals. It was going to roll over people.

"It's about time the United States government realized it can't come in here and push us around anymore. Get its murderous chemicals off our land."

There were an awful lot of cameras focused on her. All of them but one, and it was focused on Remo, who smiled at it and gave the peace sign. The camera turned away. Apparently it was getting some sort of crowd shot.

The spokesperson announced that she was not going to give any more interviews because everyone had driven several hundred miles to tell the government to get off their land and they were all very tired.

"No," she said. "I'm not an Indian and I don't live here. But I do live in this world. And even though I am Kim Kiley, actress and star, I feel I owe the world my presence here. Poison gas does not discriminate about whose lungs it tears up. Women, children, the lame, crippled, insane, drug dependent, blacks and Hispanics. And yes, famous stars whose multimillion-dollar-gross movie is appearing now at all your neighborhood film theaters. It was beautifully filmed on exotic locations. *Star Lust.* At neighborhood theaters now, starring Kim Kiley. I."

So that was why he recognized her. Behind one of the cars, a sharpshooter leveled a scope-sighted rifle at the thin man in the black T-shirt and black chinos. He aimed at the feet.

Remo thought the man could have held up a lollipop and still advertised that he was trying to shoot someone. His entire body was tensed, as if it were in pain. Remo saw the light of the gun muzzle, the line of the bullet, and moved out of its low path as it kicked up dust in the land of the Pakeeta reservation. Then came the crack of the sound catching up. The man fired again, this time at Remo's chest.

The bullet sang into the iron doors where the lead splattered with sledgehammer force. Two other gunmen joined, each behind one of the cars in the circle, putting Remo in a crossfire. Now they were aiming at him, not his feet.

Now there was yelling and screaming from the demonstrators who, as it always happened, looked for gunfire a good two seconds after the sound of the first shot. They saw the bullets kicking up dust. They saw a figure in dark shirt and slacks seem to writhe in the rain of fire and as if he were dust himself somehow move across the prairie grass like a wave, a wave that the gunfire could not quite catch.

Suddenly, as if the rifles were useless, the three

snipers threw them to the ground. Each drew a .357 Magnum from his belt.

They were large handguns, whose bullets could shoot out the support beam in a bungalow. While some bullets could go through a car door, a .357 Magnum could take it off. Each gunman knew that at close range with a slug that big, they had only to hit part of their target to disable him. A .357 Magnum bullet could catch a leg with such force that the spine would shatter.

And each of the men had been given special shells.

"You might have some difficulty hitting him," they had been told.

"I took out the eye of a grape picker in Barcelona at a hundred yards," said one gunman.

"This is not some grape picker who has displeased his patron."

"I've shot kneecaps off running men," said another gunman.

"Good. Then you will be all the more certain to kill this one. Now I want you first to fire around him, his feet, near his head. Perhaps for several shots. Then go for the body and then if you continue to miss, I want you to use these special shells in your handguns."

All three laughed. All three took the special shells. For the kind of money they were being paid, they would have taken a tank if the man had insisted. They had met him on a yacht off

Little Exuma, a faggy kind of guy, but so were many rich Americans.

And there was that strange requirement. The American had insisted that if he found out that they had used their rifles for a close-up kill, instead of the special shells in a handgun, they would not get their special bonus.

No one asked Mr. Reginald Woburn III why he expected the victim to get close if they should miss him. In fact, after being shot at, the victim, if he weren't dead, would be running away and they would have a harder time finishing him with a pistol.

After the first intentional miss, when they were trying to hit him with rifle fire, everything happened so quickly that they didn't have time to thank their good fortune when he actually charged them. It was like their bonus running right into their hands.

They were going to be paid for every slug of the .357 ammunition that they put into his body. Each of the gunmen was sure that the skinny guy in the black T-shirt was going to end up with eighteen Magnum slugs in him. They wondered if the last bullets would have to be fired at bone fragments because that would be all that was left.

They were so intent on firing all six slugs into the skinny guy that they didn't realize none of them got off the second shot.

Out came the guns, level went the sights, squeeze went the trigger fingers and away went the heads of the gunmen. The guns exploded.

To Remo it looked as if the three had blown themselves up. He looked around. The bodies were pieces of trunks. Their heads were off somewhere, in fragments across the rolling prairie. He heard the whir of the cameras. Some women were still screaming.

Remo thought he knew what was happening.

"Everyone," he yelled. "Get out of here. Get out of here. It's going to blow. Get out of here." He immediately faded back to the entrance to the underground storage of the gas drums.

But the only ones there were the guards, lying on the ground covering their heads, their bodies in the way of the door. No one could have entered. It was not a diversion to get into the doors and shoot at the drums and explode them. The purpose of the snipers blowing themselves up had to be blowing themselves up. And there wasn't a bomb inside. Or outside. Just a bunch of people running around terrified now because he had told them to run for their lives.

And they were running. Cars were starting up. Ladies were scrambling through the grass with their shoes flying off their feet. Cameramen were diving into their vans and taking off and Remo was standing there, feeling very foolish as the two guards got up and brushed themselves off.

"What's going to blow?" asked the guards, who knew no one had entered the underground storage area.

"Nothing," said Remo.

"You shouldn't scare people like that, mister, after all the shooting and everything."

"You bastard," came the shriek of a woman's voice. It was Kim Kiley running at him. Her face was twisted, her teeth bared, and she raised a fist and then slickly moved into a nice smooth groin kick. Remo moved aside as the leg went by and caught her as she lost her balance. She had put her whole body into the kick and when her toe did not meet designated tender parts of the victim, her back headed for the ground.

Remo stopped the fall and set her right. She scratched at his face. He caught her nails in his palms and pressed them back to her sides. She spat. He ducked. She swung. He stepped aside.

"Will you stay still?" she screamed.

"Okay," said Remo and she punched his chest. He let his chest muscles receive her knuckles and she let out a yell.

"Ooooh, that was weird. It was like punching air." She wiped her punching hand off on her dress as if it had encountered something slimy.

"Ooooh," she said again and shivered. "That was awful."

"I'm sorry I made punching me unpleasant, Ms. Kiley," said Remo. He had seen one of her films and wondered at her great ability to look innocent. He had never seen her with this ferocious anger.

She punched again, this time at the head. Remo

kissed the knuckles coming at him. She didn't wipe it off, just looked at her hand wondering what had gone wrong. He should have had bloody lips by now. Her agent always bled when she punched him there and he knew karate and kung fu.

"How could you do this to me? How could you do it?"

"Do what?" asked Remo.

"Ruin my demonstration. How could you do it? I'm Kim Kiley out here among these smellies, a full day's drive with major networks, all three, and the cable network, and you stage that shoot-out. Really, how could you?"

"What are you talking about?"

"Those men you had shoot at you to get all the publicity. I think they're dead. With three dead men, you could have gotten the same publicity on Hollywood and Vine. You didn't have to come out here. I came out here. I had to use the poison gas in there. I had to use this stinking reservation. Don't these people ever wash? I'm for Indian rights, but there are limits."

The guards, who were Indians, glowered at Kim Kiley. Kim waved them away as if their glowers were uncalled for.

"Ms. Kiley, this may come as a shock to you but I did not get myself shot at for publicity," Remo said.

"Really? Then why did you have that high-speed camera trained on you? It wasn't network and it wasn't cable because they always have those symbols on their cameras to prove they were there. No symbols, and trained on you."

"I *did* notice a camera," Remo said.

"Oh, really now. You noticed it, eh? You suddenly noticed the camera focusing on you all the time?"

"I noticed it focused on me. How did you know it was a high-speed camera?"

"Didn't you look? The film magazine. It's three times as big as the networks'. They use more film because of the high speed. Don't tell me you don't know that with a high-speed camera you can get a finer image of yourself?"

"Makes sense," said Remo. "But no, I didn't know that."

"And it was my bad side too. Who are you going to deal the footage through?"

"I'm not dealing any footage, whatever that is," Remo said.

"C'mon. When's your movie coming out?"

"I don't have a movie."

"With your looks? What are you doing here then?"

"I am," said Remo, remembering his identification, "with the Bureau of Indian Affairs."

"Those cameramen weren't from a government firm. They were a commercial company. I saw their truck."

"Did you see if the gunmen came from that truck?"

"I just saw the dust kick up and heard noise. One network got me out of focus at that point but everyone else just turned away. I think they were using zoom lenses on you. You got close-ups, maybe four, four and a half seconds. It's going network."

His face would be seen across the country. No matter, Remo thought. It would just be another face of someone being shot at. People saw so many faces, who would take note of his?

"How can you fraction seconds of camera time while everyone else is running for their lives?" Remo asked.

"I'm an actress. Are there any gunmen left where you hired those? It was a good move. It's going network. Getting shot at is network, prime time."

"I didn't hire them. In fact, they were trying to kill me," Remo said.

"Dead?"

"Yes. That sort of thing."

"Well, at least they didn't hurt your face." Kim Kiley caressed his cheeks with her palms, turning the head like a craftsman examining his work, then gave his cheek a friendly little pat. "Fine. A lovely face. Do you do anything with it?"

"I see through it, eat through it, talk through it and breathe through it."

"No, I mean anything important. I mean, are you doing any feature work? Television?"

"I'm not an actor."

"My Lord," gasped Kim Kiley, covering her mouth with a palm. "They were shooting at you."

"I thought I had been telling you that."

"Oh, this is terrible. Then what was that camera crew doing here shooting you with high-speed film?"

"I don't know. I honestly don't know." Remo looked at the dust on the horizon. The crews were long gone now, but perhaps the networks had accidentally gotten a shot of those cameramen who were interested in Remo. There had been cameramen too when the President had been attacked. He could have been killed anytime, but only when there were cameras present was he attacked. "Do you remember anything else about those men with the high-speed cameras?" asked Remo. He moved the actress away from the guards. Off in the distance, he heard sirens. Police must have been notified.

"Certainly," she said. "I wanted to buy some footage even though it wasn't my best side. It was Wonder Film, Palo Alto. I know them. They're reputable. They would never be involved in a shooting. They won't even film soft porn."

"Wonder Films? Sounds like a porn shop to me," said Remo.

"No. William and Ethel Wonder. They've been in the business for years. Totally reliable, totally honest. They almost went bankrupt a half-dozen times."

"Maybe they needed the money?"

"No. They can't be bought. Not everyone wants to deal with them. You know how eerie it is to know that the person you're dealing with has some things that he won't do for money. It makes my skin crawl."

"Thank you and good-bye," said Remo, glancing at the police cruisers racing down the dirt prairie road like the cavalry.

"Where are you going?" said Kim. "Cops don't pay for a personal appearance."

"I've got business. Good-bye."

"Well, so do I. I want that footage. Are you going there?" she asked.

"If I find it, I'll get it for you," Remo said.

"You wouldn't know what you're looking for. Besides, if there are going to be people shooting, I want a man around. Especially one with a nice face. What's your name?"

"Remo."

Kim Kiley squeezed his cheeks with her fingers as if she had the face of a baby in her hands.

"You really shouldn't waste that face, Remo."

"William Wonder?" said Remo. "Wonder. That's a funny name."

"And Remo isn't?"

Ethel Wonder didn't like what was going on. Even if William had never told her, she would have known it was his crazy family.

"It's not crazy, Ethel. Do I call it crazy when your family takes an infant boy and cuts off part of his pecker?"

"We've been doing it for thousands of years, William. It's a tradition."

"Well, so have we," said William Wonder. The film was being flown back to Palo Alto from the Pakeeta reservation outside Billings, Montana, by private jet. Wonder had the processing ready and refused to work on any other film until that arrived. The developing system had to be at the ready. He looked at his watch.

"I never heard of your traditions," Ethel said. "Nobody I know has ever heard of your traditions either."

"We like to keep to ourselves."

"And your family meetings. I swear. A zoo."

"We went to one family meeting."

"I remember. The western United States. Who takes a family and divides up the world?" asked Ethel Wonder. She was a plump middle-aged woman who wore too-heavy makeup and a permanent frown. Sometimes she would smile when something really amused her but nothing had amused her since the television show *Howdy Doody*.

"*Howdy Doody*, that was real humor," she said.

William's family was not real humor. It wasn't even a real family. There wasn't any warmth and many of them didn't even share the same name, and they were all different races and religions.

A writer had once said that relatives were like people you met in an elevator. You had no choice about them. William's family was exactly like people you met in an elevator. Strangers. Of course, if you ran into financial difficulty, they would help you out. They did that well.

Of course, Ethel had always made sure she paid back the loans, with interest. She didn't like that bunch. The only good thing about them was that they didn't meet often. Maybe once every fifteen or twenty years. She was not quite sure what went on there, but whatever did, she was not a part of it.

She loved William because in every other matter, he was a man she could respect. His word was iron; his life frugal and honest. And he didn't watch silly television shows.

But then his family got involved in their business and they were doing crazy things.

They had their best photographer shoot a presidential press conference at high speed. The kind of high speed you would use to stop a bullet in flight.

"Listen, William," Ethel had said. "I know the President can talk fast, but faster than a speeding bullet?"

"Ethel, it's family," William had answered. And that was supposed to settle things. The film was jetted back from Washington, processed and then jetted right out of Palo Alto again to a destination that had been kept from her.

And now again. All the development equipment was idle waiting for the film from Montana and Ethel told William:

"Crazy. I think I am going to burn that film when it comes in and tell your family to go swim in a sewer."

"Ethel, please," William said. There was sudden fear in his eyes.

"All right, all right, let's not do this again though," she said. She couldn't remember when she had seen him that frightened.

The film came from the airport by motorcycle and the cyclist waited. She went into the developing area to help her husband, who had dismissed his entire staff for the day, just as he had after the presidential press conference.

This film, too, had an attempted killing. And it too had a strange focus. When they had shot the presidential film, the object was not the President but a broad general area around him, including the reporters.

This time, there was another attempted death. By gun. They were shooting at a man in a dark T-shirt, but they didn't hurt him. It looked like a dance he did, as though he flowed with the air. He would move and then the bullet would be by him. She knew it was a bullet because it made that sort of fuzzy line a bullet would make.

Then there were no more bullets and the ground seemed to shake. Someone had set off an explosion out of range of the camera. She could see the shock waves flapping at the black T-shirt.

And then there was no more film. William examined it once more, then put it in the can and gave it to the cyclist.

"Crazy," said Ethel.

Then Kim Kiley and the man in the film came to the studio. It couldn't have been more than three hours after the cyclist left.

"Uh-oh," said Ethel. She looked to William.

"It's all right," he whispered.

"What's all right?"

"Everything," he said.

And then she heard William lie. She had never heard him lie like that before. Yes, the film was being processed right now. Could they wait a few moments and have a cup of tea with him and his wife, Ethel?

William, who would set foot in the kitchen only if he were passing out from hunger, made the tea himself.

"It doesn't have caffeine," he said. "It's a refreshing herbal essence. A beautiful fragrance."

Ethel glanced at the tea suspiciously. William liked coffee and he liked it with caffeine. It did smell wonderful though, like roses and honey, a most delicious bouquet.

He nodded for her to drink it. Kim Kiley and the man with her refused the tea. Ethel wondered

what they were going to do when the man found
out they had no film.

William nodded again for her to drink. They
both sipped. It was that sort of sweet taste that
she knew would not cling, but only refresh. It sent
a warming tingle through her body and she put
her cup down and asked to leave the world.

Why had she said that? she wondered. "Oh
yes," came the very gentle thought. "I'm dying."

Remo and Kim Kiley watched the couple smile
pleasantly, lean forward and then keep on
leaning.

"They're dead," gasped Kim. "Really dead.
Check."

"They're dead," said Remo.

"Don't you do a pulse?" she asked.

"They're dead," said Remo.

"Did they kill themselves? That's a stupid
question, right?"

"No," said Remo. "I don't think they knew
what was in that tea."

"What are you, a mind reader?"

"No," said Remo. "I read people."

"They're so still," said Kim with a shiver.

"That's what dead looks like," Remo said.

They searched the lab but could not find the
film. Kim pointed out that the developer had just
been used because the agitation baths were still at
their precise temperature.

Another strange thing was that this laboratory

usually had fifteen people working in it but when they had arrived there had been only the two owners.

"I think there has to be something special when the owners dismiss everyone and then develop the film themselves. In the old days when porn was illegal, that's how they made dirty pictures. Not this place, of course. Other small labs."

"But what's illegal about photographing me?" Remo asked.

"I think someone is trying to kill you and take pictures of it. Maybe someone wants to see you die horribly."

"In high speed?" Remo asked.

"You're a funny guy," said Kim. "Good-looking and funny."

Inside the office, they found a log of assignments. Remo noticed the same photographer who had been at the presidential press conference also shot the Billings, Montana, scene. The next assignment for Jim Worthman was the Gowata caves on the island of Pim. Jim Worthman was supposed to get footage of bat droppings.

"Bat droppings?" asked Kim. "What's the action in bat poop? I mean, doesn't it just poop?"

Remo looked at the name again. Worthman. And there was Wonder. Something in the names reminded him of something, something about other names he had been hearing.

But he didn't know what it was.

Kim shivered. She wanted to get out of this place of death. She did not approve of death and intended to delay hers as long as possible.

"I guess that's why I'm against chemicals. Really, it's a cause I am deeply devoted to."

"If you're going to come with me," Remo said, "I don't want to hear about your deepest principles."

"How do you know I want to come with you? Mind reading again?" Kim looked up and smiled.

"I have a mystic sense of a person's intentions," said Remo. "Especially when for the first time this afternoon, she just moved her eyes above my belt buckle."

Chapter Seven

Reginald Woburn III saw the film. He saw the bullets and he saw the movements. The film was fed into a computer. The computer calculated the speed of the bullet, the time of the bullet, and it told Reginald Woburn that the plum he was supposed to pluck had to be moving before the bullet left the barrel. The plum seemed to move, virtually on the sniper's decision to fire.

Stick drawings analyzed the movements of the body. They compared the movements to those of the top athletes in the world. The highest score so far in this concept of perfect movement had been a 4.7 by an Indian fakir who had chosen to compete in the Olympics ten years earlier. He had won the marathon run in a record time that had never been approached since then.

This plum, this white man named Remo, registered a 10. Reginald looked at the numbers, shut down the machine, went into the bathroom and vomited in fear.

It was almost dawn when he realized that he was actually doing everything right. The seventh stone was correct. For the great secret of the seventh stone was that the other six methods had failed. Therefore the Korean of the time of Prince Wo, that assassin from Sinanju, could not be killed by sword or poison or the other four ways. The seventh stone had said, "Do not use methods that fail." Of course, that was obvious. But when one thought about it, when one understood the stone, one realized that it was not that obvious. The way of the seventh stone was to find the way, perhaps the most mysterious of all, especially in the light of this Remo's extraordinary powers. And if *he* had such powers, what kind did the old Korean possess?

"He will show you how to kill him. Be patient and let him." That was another message from the seventh stone.

But how? Reggie didn't know, and so to find out how, he first had to find out, and to understand, how not.

Reggie went back to the bathroom and retched again. He had not expected it to go this far. He had believed that at least one bullet would work. But he had taken precautions, even if he didn't think he would need them.

The awful sense of seeing how easily the plum had avoided the first death and the magnitude of the man's abilities terrified Reggie. He trembled as he looked at the stone's message again. *Let him show you how to kill him.*

But what if he escapes again? Reggie thought. What if the great sea itself does not work?

What so worried Woburn this dark night of his soul was that he had been sure that if bullets did not work, he would find some way to pluck his plum. But the film showed nothing, no weakness. What if they could not be killed? That little house of assassins had been around for thousands of years. What if they were immortal?

Reginald Woburn III went to the beach his ancestor had landed on and in the old prayers asked the sea which had given Prince Wo safe passage once, to swallow the first plum. Because if it did, that would make the second easier to pluck.

The prayer made him feel better and what actually made his blood run fresh with vigor was his father, who had never really been easy to get along with.

Dad would not let another Wo be killed. He was vehement about that.

"Where are you talking from?" Reggie asked. Dad had reached him on the private phone, that one that could not be tapped into.

"From our Palm Beach home," his father said.

"Is Drake, the butler, there?"

"Yes. He's right behind me."

"Would you do me a favor, Dad?"

"Only if you promise not to get any more of us killed. The family is up in arms."

"I promise, Dad," Reggie said.

"All right," came the father's voice.

"Tell Drake the muffins are ready."

"The muffins are ready?"

"Yes."

"That's really silly," Reggie's father said.

"C'mon Dad. I don't have all day. Do you want my promise or not?"

"Just a minute. Drake, the muffins are ready . . . . Drake. What are you doing with that pistol? . . . Drake, put it down now or you are dismissed."

There was a crack of a shot over the telephone line.

"Thank you, Drake," Reggie said. "That will be all."

He whistled happily. He always felt good after something worked. He had discovered this wonderful ability to make things work, which really was making people work. Infinitely more delicate and rewarding than polo. And you scored in the real game of life and death. He loved this and felt the great joy of knowing he was going to be very busy from now on. He would trust the seventh stone. It had known for millennia what Reggie was just trying to discover now.

Chapter Eight

There were a lot of telephones in the airport but each seemed to have a caller permanently attached to the receiver, as if they'd come that way, packaged for delivery, straight off the assembly line.

Remo hovered around the phone bank waiting. One white-haired woman with a bright flowered dress and carrying a paper shopping bag seemed determined to reach out and touch everyone she had ever met. While Remo was waiting, she made call after call and on each one of the calls she told the same dumb stories of how her grandchildren were doing in college. Remo thought for a moment that he had found the real Ma Bell, live and in the flesh. He also thought for a moment that a good thing to do would be to pick her up bodily and go stand her behind the engine of a jet plane. He was moving toward her to do just that when he stopped himself.

What was happening to him? Why this free-floating irritation, always so close to the surface? Waiting for a telephone shouldn't have bothered him at all. Among the many things of Sinanju he had learned was patience, basic beginner's stuff, as elementary as an indrawn breath or the correct positioning of the body in accordance with the prevailing winds.

It shouldn't have bothered him now but it did. Just like the palm tree, the concrete steps and the rice. Something was happening to him and he didn't like it. He didn't like the way he was attracted to Kim Kiley. Chiun had long ago taught Remo the thirty-seven steps to bringing women to sexual ecstasy, and in learning the details, Remo had lost the desire. But now he wanted Kim Kiley, as a man wants a woman, and that annoyed him also. Too many things were annoying him these days.

He forced himself to wait in line patiently until Ma Bell finally ran out of relatives to harangue. She hung up the receiver and stood there as if searching her memory for one more name, one more telephone number. Remo reached across her and dropped a dime into the receiver and said with a sweet smile, "Thank you, Ma," and slowly edged her away from the phone.

"Ma, my ass," the woman said. "Who are you to call me Ma?"

"The guy who didn't stuff you into a jet engine,

lady. Take a hike," Remo said. So much for niceness.

After three more tries, he got Harold W. Smith on the phone.

"There wasn't any bomb," Remo said.

"No bomb," Smith repeated. Remo could almost see the frown lines deepening at the corners of his thin mouth.

"There were a couple of Pakeeta Indians though," Remo said. "They're the ones who got the Rangers."

"And?"

"I got them," Remo said. "They were waiting inside the cave to kill me." Remo thought that news might perk Smith up a bit. It wasn't a bomb to destroy America but at least it was something.

"Why? Who hired them?"

"They didn't know. They got an anonymous phone call and some cash in the mail. Somebody promised them ten grand for me and another hundred grand for describing exactly how they did it. But they didn't collect. Then there were three more incompetents waiting for me outside the cave. They fired rifles at me for a while and then they used handguns and they blew themselves up. I didn't get a chance to talk to them, but I figure their employer wasn't exactly trustworthy either."

"I saw it on television," Smith said.

"How'd I look? Somebody told me I should be in movies," Remo said.

"I guess you were moving too fast for the cameras," Smith said. "You always seemed to be a blur. You know, Remo, this is really strange."

"No, it's not. I can always be a blur when I want to," Remo said.

"I don't mean that," Smith said. "First an attempt on the President's life. Then an elaborate bomb threat that turns out to be a hoax. And both incidents staged with enough time to allow us to respond." He paused a moment. "Remo, do you think that perhaps these things happened just to try to flush you out in the open?"

"Could be," Remo said. "I told you, somebody thinks I ought to be a movie star. Maybe people just like to look at me."

"But why didn't anybody try to kill you at the President's news conference then, if they tried out at the Indian reservation?"

Remo thought a moment, then said, "Maybe somebody was trying to film me. That happened at the reservation. The networks were there, but there was also an independent film crew. They took pictures of me and the self-detonating hitmen. Super-speed film," he said. Remo went on to explain about his meeting with the late William and Ethel Wonder, the missing film and the odd coincidence that the same cameraman had covered both the news conferences and the demonstration in Montana.

"I think you're right," Smith said. "I think someone is trying to get your moves on film so that they can figure you a way to gun you down."

"Gun me down? You've been watching gangster movies again," Remo said.

"Take a vacation," Smith said, "while I figure this out."

"I already took one. Four fun-filled days of surf, sand and sun."

"Take another one. Go back to Little Exuma. You're a property owner now. Go check your property," Smith said. "Inspect your condominium."

"I don't need another vacation. I'm still recovering from the last one."

"It's not a suggestion, Remo. It's an order. Go back to Little Exuma. If you don't want to rest, don't rest, but just stay out of the way while I try to find out who's after you. Please," Smith said, and then gently cradled the receiver.

At the other end of the line, Remo listened to the pleasant humming noise for a moment, then hung up the phone. Why had Smitty been so upset? People were always trying to kill Remo. Why worry so much about a few inept would-be assassins and a missing canister of high-speed film?

It was Smitty who really needed to take a vacation. Remo didn't.

He made his way through the crowded airport to the cocktail lounge where Kim Kiley was waiting for him. She was sitting in a back booth, staring thoughtfully into a wineglass as if it

might, in some small way, hold a portent of things
to come.

When she saw him approaching, she looked up
and smiled at him with a smile so warm, so
beckoning that Remo felt a tingling in his body
that was so old, it was now new.

As he sat down, she said, "I wish we could run
away for a while together."

"How does Little Exuma sound to you?" Remo
asked.

"It sounds fine as long as it includes you."

"Okay. It's agreed," Remo said. "Little
Exuma."

"I can work on my tan," Kim Kiley said.

"You can work on my tan too," Remo said and
Kim reached across the table and gently brushed
his cheek with her fingertips.

"I'm looking forward to working on your tan.
And other things," she said.

The ink-charged brush moved across the parchment, forming the necessary characters with
strokes as sure and smooth as the movement of a
seabird's wing. Smiling, Chiun studied the page.
He had finally done it, finally managed to include
in the ongoing history of Sinanju all that was
necessary to tell about Remo and his origins. The
eyes and the skin color had been giving him
problems, but he had solved that with a pair of
master strokes. He had written that Remo had a

certain roundness of eye which was regarded as attractive by many people in the world who suffered from the round-eye affliction.

This, Chiun had said, made Remo a definite asset when seeking contracts in many places in the world because these round-eyed things like to deal with one who resembles their own kind. Chiun was proud of himself for turning a negative into a positive.

And Remo's skin color? Chiun had solved that even more easily. From now on, in the histories of Sinanju, Remo would be referred to as "Remo the Fair."

There. It was written. All the facts were there for anyone to see and he, Chiun, could not be blamed if some future Master of Sinanju was unable to see the truth inside the truth.

With a sigh of satisfaction, Chiun put down the bamboo-handled brush. Someday, he thought, he would find a truly satisfactory way of dealing with Remo's birthplace. He would find a way of writing Newark, New Jersey, to make it sound as if it were part of Sinanju. But that would be later.

He broke off his reverie as he saw two figures advancing up the sun-swept beach. Remo was back and that was good. But there was a young woman with him and that was not good at all.

This was the hiding time and Remo, as a new Master, should withdraw from the world for a while, and that meant withdrawing from people

too. The hiding time would not last much longer;
Chiun was sure of that. But it should not be
ignored. Remo just did not understand.

"Little Father, I'm back."

"Yes, you are back." Chiun glanced beyond
Remo to the girl who lingered at the edge of the
beach.

"I brought a friend along."

"A friend," Chiun sputtered. "And what am
I?"

"All right, I'll play your silly game," Remo
said. "What are you?"

"She is your friend, and I? A millstone around
your neck, no doubt. An incurable disease. Some
old robe, fraying at the edges, to be cast on the
trash heap without a moment's thought."

Remo sighed. "You are my friend, Little
Father, as you know. And as you know, you are a
great deal more. And you are also, at times, a
giant-sized pain in my rear end."

Chiun moaned. "Words to pierce an old man's
heart." His thin voice quavered. "It is not enough
that I have given you Sinanju? Devoted my best
years to your training and well-being?" There was
a rustle of silk as he raised one frail-looking hand
to his forehead in a gesture that Sarah Bernhardt
would have loved. "It is obviously not enough for
you, however."

"I said you were my friend."

"Well, if I am your friend, why do you have to
have another one?"

"Because she's a different kind of friend. There isn't any law that says I can't have more than one friend. Her name is Kim Kiley and you might even like her if you give her half a chance."

"This is not the time for new friendship." Chiun's tone was grave, his hazel eyes solemn. "You must rest for a while. You should study the scrolls and practice and nothing more. Scrolls are restful. Practice is restful. Women, as all know, are not restful. They are fickle and frivolous. That one has already vanished."

Remo didn't bother to turn around. "She said she was going to walk along the beach while I talked to you. She'll be back in a while."

"Perhaps the sea will swallow her up."

"I wouldn't get my hopes up," Remo said.

"What good is a friend if you do not heed his advice? Send her away."

"She just got here," Remo said.

"Perfect," Chiun said, nodding to himself as he agreed with himself. "Then she can go away before she gets comfortable. Then you and I can have a good vacation."

Remo could feel it again, that restless impatience building up inside him. The urge to break things for no other reason than to see if the separate pieces were more interesting than the whole thing.

"I'm going for a walk on the beach," Remo said abruptly. "I let you and Smitty con me into coming down here in the first place. Now with

Kim here for company, maybe I can have a good
time. Just think, Little Father. Maybe we'll find
out a new way to counteract the hiding period.
You can write it in your histories and the next
five thousand years of Sinanju will love you for
it."

"Go ahead," Chiun snapped. "Go. No need to
tell me where you're going. I'll just sit here by
myself. Alone. In the dark. Like some old ripped
sock no longer worth the mending."

Remo decided not to point out that it wouldn't
be dark for four more hours yet. He called over his
shoulder as he walked away: "Whatever makes
you happy. And I know that misery usually does."

Chiun's hazel eyes followed Remo until he disappeared around the curve of the white sand
beach. He wished that he could make Remo
understand, but Remo had not grown up in the
village of Sinanju. He had never played the hiding
game, never prepared himself for the time when
his instincts would have to be stronger than his
mind or even his heart. Remo had grown up
playing a game called "stickball." Chiun wondered what major challenge of adult life "stickball" prepared you for. Even if you could, as
Remo contended, hit the ball four sewers. Whatever that was.

Sighing again, Chiun looked back down at the
scroll. There was nothing he could do for Remo,
nothing but watch and wait until the hiding time

had passed. This was not, Chiun decided, a good vacation at all.

Remo watched as Kim moved toward him, running coltishly through the surf, her dark hair windblown and free, her long shapely legs churning up the shallow water. She looked innocent and tomboyish with her pants rolled up and her shirttail loose and flapping. She looked like the Kim Kiley he remembered from the movies.

"I found this great cave," she called out breathlessly. A few seconds later, she wrapped her arms around Remo's neck, lightly brushed her lips against his and then, tugging at his hand, led him along the beach like a child's toy on a string.

"You've got to see it," she said. "The sun and the water make these crazy beautiful patterns on the ceiling. It's worth the whole trip here, it's so beautiful."

"You ought to give guided tours," said Remo.

"You're getting the first, last and only one. The one with all the personal extras thrown in at no additional charge."

"I like the sound of that," said Remo, who did.

"You'd better," she warned him with a gamin grin. She linked her arm through Remo's and led him over the rocks and along a strip of narrow beach.

"There it is." She pointed toward the back of the deserted cove. The entrance to the cave was a

jagged, mouth-shaped opening in the side of a
sheer-faced cliff. It seemed to beckon them, to
pull them in of its own accord like the gaping
hungry maw of some prehistoric predator who,
despite the passage of ages, had never lost its
appetite.

Chiun found it soothing to talk to someone who
not only listened but seemed to hang on his every
word. Here at last was a white man who re-
spected age and wisdom. In other words, someone
not at all like Remo.

"I saw your friend just a few minutes ago,"
Reginald Woburn III said when Chiun finished a
lengthy speech on ingratitude. "He was walking
with a pretty girl toward the caves at the far end
of the island."

"What a way to spend a vacation," Chiun
sighed. "Walking on the beach with a beautiful
woman. If he would only listen to me, we could
be having a really good time."

"I only mentioned it because those caves can be
pretty dangerous. Very pretty scenery when the
tide is out but a real death trap when it starts
pouring back in. It's nearly impossible to swim
out against the onrushing tide. They lost a couple
of tourists there early this season. Found the
bodies the next morning, all gray and bloated.
Fish ate the eyes out." Reggie's smile broadened as
he listed the details. "Would have put a real
crimp in the tourist business if they hadn't taken

the bodies and dumped them over on Martinique. The couple was on the Buena Budget Excursion Special and Martinique was their next stop anyway. But they died here."

"An old Korean proverb," Chiun said. "When death speaks, everyone listens."

"But I am worried about your friends," Reggie said.

"Why?" Chiun frowned.

"The tide *could* trap them in one of those caves," Reggie said, warming to his subject. "They wouldn't realize it until it was too late. They'd be fighting an oncoming wall of water, swimming helplessly, hopelessly against the tide. Holding their breaths until their faces turned color and their lungs burst from the strain. They'd float around for a while, their bodies battering against the rocks. Then the fish would start on them. Nibble here, small bite there. They always seem to go for the eyes first. And then if there's enough blood in the water, they might get sharks. With those big jaws that tear off limbs the way we snap a celery stalk. Then you'd really see action. The sea would turn a dark purple red and be churning. A feeding frenzy." Reggie sighed. Little drops of spittle clung to the corners of his mouth. His heart was thundering as if he were a marathon runner approaching the finish line. He felt a warmth in his groin that even sex couldn't rival. "I can see it all quite clearly. It could very easily happen to your friends."

"That woman is no friend of mine," Chiun snapped.

"What about the man?"

Chiun was thinking. "I suppose a person could get killed that way. If he were truly stupid."

"Then what about your friend?" Reggie said again.

"Remo has his moments," said Chiun. "But even he isn't that stupid."

Chapter Nine

"Am I the most beautiful woman you've ever known?" Kim whispered softly.

She lay snuggled in the crook of Remo's arm, the two of them naked on the warm gritty sand inside the cave, watching the fantastic light show provided by the setting sun as its multicolored rainbow rays were reflected off the clear blue water. It was cool and dry in the cave and the sound of the waves against the distant rocks was better than any soundtrack Hollywood had ever come up with.

After a long silent minute, Kim frowned and poked Remo in the ribs. "That was supposed to be an easy question. And don't you tell me you're thinking about it."

Remo ruffled her dark lustrous hair. "You're the most beautiful woman I've ever known," he said.

Kim smiled. "Everybody tells me that."

"Who's everybody?" It was one of those things that Remo wondered about every now and again. How many bodies did it take to make an everybody?

"You know. Everybody. Friends, admirers, agents, producers and directors." She counted them off, one by one, on her long slender fingers. "And of course my thousands of loyal and devoted fans. I get over five hundred letters a week that say they love me."

"You answer them?" Remo was curious. He never got any mail. Even when he was alive, no one wrote to him, and now that he was supposed to be dead, the mail hadn't changed. Chiun had once, by mistake, rented a post-office box in Secaucus, New Jersey, but all the mail that came had been addressed to Chiun and he wouldn't show Remo any of it.

Kim was laughing. "Answer the mail? Are you crazy? Who's got time for that crapola? I'm not going to risk writer's cramp just to make some yahoo's day. I did answer some fan letters years ago when I was just starting out and you know what happened?"

"No."

"I broke a goddamned nail. It hurt like hell and it was months before they were all the same length again." She nestled closer to Remo, her full perfect breasts brushing against his chest. Remo touched her hand to his lips and kissed her fingernails. It was a small gesture but he could feel Kim Kiley tremble.

"It was a harrowing experience," she said. "I'm just not into self-destruction. The writing was bad enough, but that wasn't all. You just try licking a couple of rolls of stamps sometime. It makes your tongue feel like something furry curled up and died on it."

"Then you don't answer your fan mail, at all?"

"Sure I do. I've got this service that takes care of it. Yours Truly Incorporated. They handle all the big stars' mail. They've got this room full of old ladies who just sit there signing letters all day long. It's a great system." Kim grinned. "They sign the junk mail and I sign the contracts for three-picture deals. What could be fairer than that?"

"Nothing, I guess," Remo said. "But I think if anybody ever wrote me a letter, I'd answer it myself."

"Well, that's you," Kim said. She smiled at him, then began to move her long shapely legs, wrapping one around Remo's while she slowly moved the other back and forth over his groin in a gentle massaging motion. Remo lay there still, smiling like a big cat on a sunny windowsill, enjoying it much too much, but doing nothing to respond.

This vacation stuff wasn't so bad after all, he thought. He felt an odd contentment, a loosening

of his inner control, and while Chiun might find
that dangerous and perhaps it was in most
contexts, right now it allowed Remo to really
enjoy the warm silky texture of the body molded
to his, the play of Kim's busy hands and legs as she
strove to please him. Remo stirred, stretched and
pulled her gently on top of him. Kim let out a low
moan as their two bodies melded together in a
fire-flash of pure energy.

The scent of her perfume filled Remo's nostrils
with an essence of dark primal earth. He had a
sudden vision of a stone altar in a shadow-
dappled jungle clearing, sunlight filtering
through the treetops and bright tropical flowers
growing beside a clear blue stream. The scent was
a heady mixture of musk and oils and spices.

Gently, Remo made their bodies into one. Kim
drew a long shuddery breath and held him tight.

"Nothing like this before," she said. "Nothing
like this."

"Don't talk," Remo said.

"It's like drugs," she said. "It's too high."

"Shhhh," said Remo.

"It's wing walking," she said.

"Don't say anything. Listen to the waves,"
Remo said. Through a few strands of ebon hair,
Remo could see the last of the setting sun. The
cooling breeze that filled the cave was heavy with
salt and the gentle murmur of the waves had
grown to a deep-throated thundering.

"Waves turn me on," Kim shouted but the words were scarcely audible as they were swallowed up by the furious pounding of the surf. She clung to Remo, her supple body shuddering slightly like a reed in a breeze. She parted her full lips and released a sound between a sigh and a moan and Remo stayed with her and pulled her closer and the sound turned to a long scream. Her body turned atop him and she lay there for a long minute before she eased herself free and rolled off Remo and stretched out on the sand beside him again.

He turned to her and she said something but he could not hear the words as the sound of the sea filled the cave like the blood-lust roar of the crowd in an ancient Roman arena.

Remo saw a shadow of fear cloud the placid expression on her beautiful face. As she struggled to her feet, Remo turned and saw it coming toward them—a solid towering wall of water that blocked out the last of the dying sun and filled the mouth of the cave with its ominous fury. It came rushing toward them, all the power of the uncaring sea channeled by the narrow walls of the cave, a destructive force that would smash them against the rocks, battered, bloody and broken, gasping for one last breath before the briny sea water filled their lungs.

Remo stood, turned and reached for Kim's hand. But she had panicked and bolted toward the back of the cave. Remo shouted for her to stop but the words were lost, drowned out by the all-enveloping growl of the hungry sea.

Mouthing a curse, Remo reached her with two long strides and scooped her up in his arms. She screamed soundlessly and beat against his chest with her fists, struggling to free herself. Ignoring her, Remo concentrated on the sound beneath the deafening roar, the smaller noises the water made as it passed across the rock, the sounds that indicated the true way of its movement and force.

He held Kim Kiley tightly and angled his body to the curve of the wave as the cold dark water took them for its own. Pushing off the sandy floor of the cave, Remo turned slowly, riding the tremendous pull of the incoming tide. It carried them for a brief moment farther into the narrowing rock-edged maw of the cave. Remo listened and waited, sensing, judging, timing the next move because if it was done incorrectly, it would leave them as nothing more than shattered lifeless pulp. He sensed, then saw a slight rise in the roof of the cavern. As they were swept beneath it, he dived deep, below the bone-crushing force of the water. A split second before they would have reached bottom, Remo pulled gracefully out of the dive.

He could feel pressure on his lungs as he kicked off the sandy floor and began to work his way back toward the entrance. He had outmaneuvered the deadly tidal trap but in doing so had placed them even further away from fresh air and freedom. Kim continued to struggle in his arms but there was a sluggishness to her movements and little force behind her tight-fisted blows. Remo hoped that she had enough air to last until they broke the surface. From the blueing tinge of her skin and her wild expression of desperation, it was going to be a close call.

Remo heron-kicked them through the dark murky water. If he could use his arms, he could have them out of there in seconds, but to free his arms he would have to release Kim.

There was no light in the water-filled cave but Remo could see clearly enough to follow in the direction where the water grew lighter. He saw, as he passed great tangled webs of seaweed, sharp rocks and carrion fish, all teeth and eyes that seemed to measure the two humans in terms of bite per pound.

One of the fish, a long silvery creature that looked like the Goodyear blimp after a diet, darted in close and took a tentative nip at Remo's arm. Remo angled slightly away, back-kicked and pushed forward. The big silver fish slammed against the rock wall. Its body crumpled and it dropped toward the ocean floor, spreading a trail of blood behind it. The other fish gave up on Remo and homed in on their comrade. For a moment the turbulence of their feeding frenzy was greater than the onrushing tide and the water churned and bubbled, a pinkish frothy white as they fought each other for the right to eat the last of their companion.

As they reached the gap-toothed entrance to the cave, Remo felt Kim go limp in his arms. Her face was greenish and bloated and her dark eyes seemed ready to pop out of her head. Scissoring his legs, Remo hurriedly propelled them toward the light and air above, ignoring the pull of the current that tried to suck them back into the cave. Their heads broke the water's choppy surface and Remo slapped Kim on the back. Sputtering, she coughed up a bilious string of seawater and gasped for air for her oxygen-starved lungs. Then Remo just held her for a time above the crested wave of the incoming tide. Gradually, her breathing became more normal and the hint of a rosy natural glow began to return to her face.

"We've got to stop hanging out in dives," Remo said. "You okay?"

"I'm alive." Kim managed a faint smile. "But I do have this uncontrollable desire to be back on dry land."

"No problem," Remo said. "Just lean back and relax." Locking his arms around her, he let the tide carry them both back to shore. He lifted her out of the pounding surf and carried her over the slippery rocks, finally putting her naked body down gently on the dunes above.

"I thought we were dead for sure," she said, staring at him. "How did you do that?"

"Do what?"

"Get us out of that cave swimming against the current. It's impossible to do that."

"I did it with mirrors," Remo said.

"*You're* impossible," she said with a small laugh. She slipped her arms around Remo's neck, clinging tight. Even though the night air was balmy, he could feel her shivering.

"We'd better get back," Remo said. "I think we've had enough vacation for one day. Anyway, I don't know what the dress code is around here but I don't think a well-placed hand and a couple of clam shells are going to count for too much."

"I'm ready to go back," Kim said quietly. Her teeth were chattering and her smooth skin was pebbled with goose bumps.

With his arm around her trembling shoulders, Remo led her along the dark deserted beach. There were lights on in the condominium. Chiun sat cross-legged on the floor, engrossed in one of the scrolls. As Remo shepherded Kim through the open French doors, Chiun looked up and said, "Usually I prefer that people who visit wear clothing. Particularly whites."

"We were in one of the caves down the beach," said Remo. "The tide came in and trapped us there. Swimming out was close."

Chiun shook his head. "I heard that those caves were treacherous. A number of people have drowned there, usually people who have not paid the proper amount of attention to their surroundings. People easily distracted by trivial things."

He folded his hand across his narrow chest. "I'm
not criticizing, you understand. I never criticize.
It is one of my truly outstanding qualities that no
matter how stupid you are, I never tell you about
it."

"You just keep not telling me about it," Remo
said. "I've got to do something." He slipped into
the bathroom and came out with a towel
wrapped around his middle and a fluffy white
terrycloth robe in his arms. It had the condo
resort emblem on the pocket and was five sizes too
large for Remo. The management had sent it over
after Remo's impromptu landscaping of the aloe
garden. Kim moved out from behind the thin
gauze curtain where she had been hiding and
slipped it on. It looked on her like an unpegged
tent but somehow Remo thought it made her look
gorgeous.

Chiun was still explaining how he never
criticized stupid Remo for being stupid, acting
stupidly, living his life in a stupid fashion.

"Chiun, this is Kim Kiley."

"Nice to meet you," said Kim. Along with the
pleasantry, she gave Chiun one of the megawatt
smiles that melted the hearts of moviegoers
around the world.

"Of course it's nice to meet me," Chiun replied
in Korean. He inclined his head a scant eighth of
an inch. In Sinanju, it was the form of greeting
used to acknowledge the presence of lepers, tax
collectors and traffickers in day-old fish heads. It

acknowledged their presence but completely ignored their existence. A fine point of Sinanju etiquette that was not lost on Remo.

Remo cleared his throat. "I thought since we've got plenty of room, we could put up Kim for a few days. You'd hardly notice she was here."

"I would notice she was here. And more important, so would you," Chiun said, shaking his head. "This is not a good thing. We cannot have her staying with us."

"We were just talking about your well-known generosity," Remo said.

"That's the trouble with being generous," Chiun said. "Everyone wants to take advantage of you. You give a little here, a little there and suddenly you have nothing left and you are out in the street with a frayed robe and a beggar bowl."

"Kim is from Hollywood," Remo said. "She's a movie star."

Chiun looked up with heightened interest.

"Were you ever in *As the Planet Revolves?*" he asked.

"Ugggh. A soap? No, I was never in a soap."

Chiun pursed his lips in distaste at her distaste.

"Do you know Barbra Streisand?" he asked, mentioning his favorite American woman.

"No. Not really."

"Do you know Cheeta Ching?" Chiun asked, mentioning his favorite television personality.

"No," Kim said.

"Do you know Rad Rex?" Chiun asked,

mentioning the name of his favorite soap-opera star.

"Sure," Kim said. "He's a fag."

In Korean, Chiun said, "Remo, get this imposter out of here." He looked down again at his scrolls.

Remo said, "I'd better get you a room, Kim."

"I'd rather stay with you," she said.

Remo shrugged. "I'm sorry but Chiun doesn't think that's a good idea."

"Do you always do what he says?"

"Most of the time," Remo said.

"Why?"

"Because most of the time he's right."

"I never heard of a servant who was right," Kim Kiley said.

"Chiun's not a servant."

"I thought he was. Chinese butlers are all the rage on the coast right now. They're such hard workers and you can usually get them at minimum wage. And they're really decorative and cute, padding around the house like little yellow gnomes. Do you think your friend would be interested in domestic work?"

"No." Remo grinned. "I don't think so." He tried to picture Chiun maneuvering the Electrolux over the carpet, taking out the trash, passing out a tray of canapes at a cocktail party. It seemed very improbable and when he glanced toward Chiun, the old Korean mouthed the words for "Out. Get her out of here."

"I'd better see about your room," said Remo. He pressed a buzzer in the wall and waited and in less than a minute, three men in white with red sashes around their waists appeared at the French doors. They looked nervous because they were nervous. They had waited on Remo before.

"You rang, sir?" all called in unison.

"Right. I need a room for Miss Kiley here."

"A room, sir?"

"Yes, a room. You know, one of those things with four walls."

The three knew that there weren't any rooms. Not only here at the Del Ray Bahamia but on the whole island itself. This was the height of the tourist season and there weren't any rooms. There was an oversized utility closet up on the third floor, but they didn't want to think about what would happen if they offered this man an oversized utility closet.

There was only one vacant lodging in the whole complex—the senator's suite. The senator's suite was furnished with priceless antiques and the walls were covered with Rembrandts, Van Goghs and Picassos. It had its own wine cellar and Jacuzzi.

The senator allowed no one into his permanent suite, not even the local help. He sent his own German cleaning woman down once a week by Lear jet to dust off the priceless Ming vases and fluff the pillows. If they put this woman in the senator's suite and he found out about it, they would all lose their jobs, have their tax returns audited and go to jail for the rest of their lives.

But if they told Remo no . . . They remembered the wall and the desk he had thrown through the window.

The senator was in Washington and the cleaning woman wasn't due for five more days.

"We'll put her in the senator's suite," the three said in unison.

Remo smiled. "That sounds good."

"It is good. It is the very best we have."

"I'm starved too," said Kim. "I'd like something to eat."

"Anything you want, miss."

"A filet mignon. Rare. If there isn't a little blood on the plate, I'll know it's been overcooked. And I'd like a baked potato with that, sour cream and a big salad with bleu-cheese dressing. Send a bottle of burgundy along too. The older the better."

"Will the gentleman be dining with madam?" they asked.

"Fresh water and rice," Remo said.

"Nice and clumpy," the three chorused. "Just the way you like it."

They looked to Remo for approval and Remo nodded and smiled.

Chiun grumbled in Korean for Remo's ears. "Good. Get out of here and go watch that cow eat dead cow meat."

"Sure," said Remo. If Chiun wanted to be

alone, let him be alone. Remo hadn't wanted this vacation in the first place and now that he was starting to enjoy it a little, he wasn't going to let Chiun spoil it. If only Remo could shake that crazy restless feeling that sat in him like an undigested meal. He thought he had lost it for a while, back there in the cave with Kim before the tide came in, but now it was back, clinging and unshakable as the smell of death itself.

"We'll show you to the senator's suite now," the room-service trio offered.

Kim followed them through the door, the oversized robe trailing behind her like a beachwear wedding gown. Remo paused in the doorway, turned and said, "Good night, Little Father."

"For some," Chiun muttered without looking up from the spread-out roll of parchment. "If you come back reeking of dead cow meat, you'll have to sleep on the beach."

Remo smiled. "I don't think I'll have any trouble finding a place to sleep."

Chapter Ten

Reginald Woburn III took a tentative sip of orange juice, gagged and spit it out. Fighting the queasy feeling in his stomach, he poked at the two crisp strips of bacon on his plate, but couldn't bring himself to lift them to his mouth. He knew they were fine, just the way he liked them, but right now they had no more appeal than terminal lung cancer.

And the eggs were worse. There were two of them, sunny-side-up, nestled in the center of the plate between the sliced fruit and bacon, but they stared up at him like two milky-yellow blind but accusatory eyes. He could almost hear them speaking to him: "Reginald, you failed again. What kind of Wo descendant are you? You are a failure."

Reggie pushed over the glass-and-wrought-iron table. It hit the carpeted floor of the gazebo with a crackling crash. The tabletop shattered. The glassware broke. Food bits were spattered everywhere.

Reggie shoved back his chair and ran into the shrubbery, retching, his throat constricted, flooded with the loathsome-tasting bile. He tried to throw up, but nothing came out because his stomach was as empty as a freshly dug grave.

He had not been able to eat anything, not since last evening when he heard the news that the sea had not killed the one called Remo.

This time it wasn't a couple of lazy Indians or three over-priced hit men. The sea was the goddamned sea. The sea, cold, relentless, powerful enough to swallow up fleets of ships.

But not Remo. No, the sea could suck up the *Titanic* like a cocktail hors d'oeuvre, but Remo just went right through it, from bottom to top, and swam back to shore again with no more challenge than if he had been paddling around the shallow end of a backyard pool. With the girl in tow; that made it even more incredible.

Reggie rose from his knees and brushed off his white flannel trousers. His hands were shaking as if he had just come off a three-day party at the polo club with plenteous liquor and pliable women.

He moved slowly, like an old man with aching legs and nowhere to go, back to the gazebo, and collapsed into the high-backed wicker chair. Deep down inside, where his heart was supposed to be, he knew what was wrong with him. It wasn't that his stomach hurt or his hands trembled. They were symptoms. What was wrong with him was fear, terror, older and darker than time itself. He could feel it eating away at him, consuming him in big hungry mouthfuls from the inside out, and he didn't know how much longer he would be able to stand it. Soon, nothing would be left but a dry empty husk, not enough Reggie Woburn left beneath the dry papery skin to even matter.

Could it be that the seventh stone was wrong? Were these two invincible? Or did he just not understand the stone's message yet?

He had been certain that the sea would kill the "plum" named Remo, so certain that he already considered it an accomplished fact. But the sea, so big that you couldn't even hire it to do your work, had failed him. And what else was left? There had to be something else, especially now that the two "plums" were together again. But as he sat and thought, no new ideas came to him, only the fear gnawing away at his insides, taking away a little more of his manhood with every passing minute.

He tried to get a grip on himself. He needed something, something big and important to prove that he was not only still a man, but also the first son of the first son in the direct line of Wo, and therefore a ruler.

His train of thought was broken by the sound of someone singing. It was a high strong lusty voice, female and thick with the island's lyrical accents. The sea breeze carried the song from the beach. It was a happy song, a celebration of love and life, and not at all the kind of song that Reggie was in the mood to hear.

Craning his neck, he peered over the thick wall of shrubbery that separated his gazebo from the beach. He saw an immense black figure waddle into view. Her brightly colored cotton dress stretched around her huge body like a sausage casing about to split. The woman's toenails were painted an improbable day-glo pink. A bright red kerchief was wrapped around her head and atop that was a towering stack of hand-woven baskets nearly as tall as herself.

She moved along the sunlit beach with her own easy, shuffling rhythm, singing. As she came abreast of the gazebo, she noticed Reggie and ended her song abruptly and favored him with a wide easy smile.

"Basket Mary at your service," she said. "Everybody know me. I make the best baskets in all the islands, maybe even the whole wide world. Big baskets, little baskets, all sizes in between, all different colors, all different shapes. You want something special, I make it up for you. Only one day wait. You ask anybody and they tell you that Basket Mary's baskets are the best. The best."

She paused at the end of her oft-practiced spiel and looked at Reginald Woburn III for encouragement.

"Let's have a look at them then," Reggie said
with a smile. He leaned over and opened the little
wrought-iron gate buried inside the shrubs and
then stepped back while Basket Mary squeezed
her bulk through it. Her grin faded a little as she
caught sight of the overturned table, the shattered
crockery, the little slumps of congealed egg and
fruit with the bluebottle flies buzzing around
them. Something was not so nice here was the expression that briefly crossed her face. Something
was not right. But like the smallest cloud crossing
in front of the sun, the feeling passed in just a
moment. Basket Mary looked up. The sun was
still there, right up in the middle of the sky as
always, and she smiled as she looked again at
Reginald Woburn and noticed his beautifully cut
clothes, the luxurious furnishings of his gazebo
and the private beach that led to the big fine
mansion on the hill behind it.

Basket Mary decided there was nothing wrong
here, at least nothing that a couple of her baskets
couldn't cure.

"Let's see the green-and-white one there,"
Reggie suggested. "The one in the middle of the
stack."

"You got the eye for real quality," Basket Mary
congratulated him. With a swift and surprisingly
graceful motion, she transferred the teetering
stack of baskets from her head to her hands and
then to the carpeted floor. She leaned over to
separate the one he wanted from the stack. Reggie

leaned over too. He was smiling as his fingers fumbled for and clasped the breakfast knife, lifting it out of the debris of his scattered food.

Suddenly Reggie was feeling good. The fear that had clawed at his inside was melting away as if it had never been there at all. In its place was a warm glow, the thrill of anticipation. What had he ever been afraid of?

"Here you go." Looking up, Basket Mary held out the pretty green-and-white basket.

"And here you go," Reggie said, smiling. Sunlight glistened off the long slender blade as he drove it into her vast chest. Blood sputtered around the metal and Basket Mary screamed, until Reggie clapped his hand over her mouth and bore her to the ground with the weight of his own body, as his knife continued to rummage around in the big woman's chest.

She struggled for a few moments, her body thudding around as she tried to buck Reggie off her. The latticework walls of the gazebo shook, and then she was still.

Reggie never felt better in his life. Suddenly, he wanted breakfast. He rose and looked down at Basket Mary's body. Then he remembered something he read once: that inside every fat person was a thin person trying to get out.

He knelt again alongside Basket Mary, raised the knife and started to test that theory.

When he was done, he picked up a telephone and dialed the police. "Could you send someone over?" he requested cheerfully. "There's a dead woman all over my gazebo."

The constable arrived an hour later. He stood just inside the wrought-iron gate and surveyed the carnage with professional calm. "No arrow in the heart, no morder," he pronounced. "Natural causes for sure. Never any morder here. Just surf, sun and good times. A real vacation paradise."

"Absolutely," Reggie agreed. He nodded toward what used to be Basket Mary. "If it's not too much trouble, I'm a little short of staff."

"No trouble," the constable said. "I get her up for you." He reached into the pocket of his baggy uniform and pulled out a folded plastic trash bag. "My scene-of-the-crime kit," he said. "Never go nowhere without it. Come in handy when these natural-causes deaths be messy like this one."

"Very commendable," Reggie said.

"You go and enjoy yourself. I clean up fine." Kneeling down on the blood-soaked carpet, he began to shove Basket Mary into the bag, with all the eagerness of a slum kid who had unintentionally been invited to the White House Easter-egg hunt.

The aftermath of killing held no interest for Reggie. He picked up a croissant that had landed atop one of the bushes, and munching casually, he opened the gate and sauntered down to the beach. There was a cool pleasant breeze from the sea. Gulls wheeled and dived above the clear blue water. The surf lapped gently against the rocks like a lover talking.

Reggie sat down on a flat-topped rock at the water's edge. Now that he was feeling like his old self again, his thoughts returned to the problem of the two plums. He could think of them now without fear. It was a strange but wonderful contentment, a feeling of being at peace with himself.

With the sun warm against his face, he leaned over to doodle in the wet sand with his blood-encrusted finger. He drew a sailing ship with no emblem on its unfurled canvas. He doodled men in armor, their faces old and wise and full of mystery. He drew himself and his father and a crude outline of the island and finally the seventh stone itself. The surf came in, spitting at the rocks. When it went back out again, the wet sand was smooth, his drawings erased by the sea.

Not fully aware of what he was doing, Reggie leaned over again. The sand and water had washed the blood from his finger. He began to draw again, not shapes or images this time, but a single word, in ancient runelike characters. He recognized the language immediately. It was the language of Wo, the words that tied all the descendants of Prince Wo together. And he recognized the word too, a single word of command that had come unbidden to his casual finger from somewhere in the deep recesses of his mind. He had known all the time what he must do about the "two plums." Smiling, Reggie stood and studied the word in the sand. It was a summons, a call to the far-flung Wo clan.

The single word was "COME."

Reggie sent the one word to the farthest corners of the earth. In Nairobi, the Wosheesha tribe forsook the sacred ritual of the harvest hunt to pack up their spears and leather thongs. In Hokkaido, Japan, the Woshimoto clan prepared their ceremonial robes and made a final visit to the graves of their ancestors. In Manchester, England, the Woosters packed their gladstones and left a note for the milkman. The Wogrooths of Holland left their tulip beds in the care of a neighbor while the Worriers of France closed and shuttered their prosperous Left Bank café.

Two mornings later, the descendants of Prince Wo had converged on the island of Little Exuma.

As the clock in the tower of Government House chimed the noon hour, Reginald Woburn III rose from his chair at the head of a long banquet table. The table was piled high with food, an international bazaar of delicacies representing the best of more than a dozen different cultures. There was even more diversity in the people seated in the high-backed chairs that bordered the table. Faces as ebony as a starless night; delicate oval faces the precise shade of yellowing ivory; bland milk-white faces, cream and cocoa faces, cinnamon-red faces; young faces and old faces, and all of them turned attentively to the man at the head of the table.

"You are all welcome here," Reginald Woburn greeted them. "You have come from near and far in answer to my summons and now we are all together, every last living descendant of the great Prince Wo. It is a time for rejoicing, a time for celebration, but that is not the only reason you have traveled these many miles."

He looked around the large room. The faces stared at him.

"We are gathered here for a purpose, a noble undertaking that will, once and for all, restore our noble house to its full and rightful position of honor. We have come here to band together against a single enemy. We are united so that we may banish him from the face of the earth forever."

"Who is this great enemy?" Maui Wosheesha demanded. His voice was as full of quiet strength as a lion passing silently through the high grass. His gold and ivory bracelets clattered musically as his broad hand closed around the shaft of his steel-tipped spear.

"You wish to see him?" Reggie asked. "You desire to hear his name spoken aloud?"

"Show the man and say the name," Hirako Woshimoto insisted. There was the faintest rustle of silk as his fingers came to rest on the tasseled handle of his ceremonial samurai sword.

"The man is one called Remo. And if you wish

to see him, you need merely to look beneath your plates."

The low-voiced murmur of a dozen different tongues accompanied the lifting of the plates. There was a photograph under each one, all alike. They showed Remo, wearing the ugly grayish suit he had worn to the presidential press conference. The camera had caught him in the instant that he had tossed a notebook, severing Du Wok's sword hand from the rest of his arm.

"His head is mine," Ree Wok shouted.

"Mine," said Maui Wosheesha.

"Mine," said Hirako Woshimoto.

Reginald Woburn silenced them with an upraised hand.

"Who will kill this man?" he shouted.

"I will." A hundred voices, a dozen tongues, all of them speaking as one. The windowpanes rattled as the chorused response filled the huge dining hall.

Reginald Woburn smiled, then slowly looked around the long table, meeting the eyes of each of them in turn.

"He who kills him will have a further honor," he said.

"What is this honor that will be mine?" asked Hirako Woshimoto.

"He who kills this man will be allowed to kill another."

"Who is?"

"The beast," Reginald Woburn said. "The Korean assassin who drove Prince Wo to these shores. For this young one is his disciple and the seventh stone tells us that both must die."

Chapter Eleven

"Pay attention now," said Chiun. "A wandering mind gathers only moss."

"That's a rolling stone," said Remo, "and I am paying attention. I always pay attention."

"You know less about attention than you know about wisdom. A rolling stone gathers *no* moss; a wandering mind gathers *all* moss. They are very different," Chiun said.

"If you say so, Chiun," Remo said. He smiled at his teacher, who looked away, annoyed. Chiun was worried about Remo. The hiding time had still not passed for him, and he was out of touch with himself and his reason for being. He did nothing now except to perform unspeakable acts with that imposter posing as an actress, who didn't even know Barbra Streisand, and that was proof that there was something wrong with Remo.

Because he should not be paying so much attention to a woman and to sex; there were more important things for a Master of Sinanju, primarily training and contemplation. As it was now, Chiun had had to implore Remo to show up for this training session.

"Watch closely now," Chiun said.

"I am watching. Is this a test to see how long I last before I collapse of boredom?"

"Enough," Chiun muttered.

They stood on the beach of a deserted inlet on the undevloped side of the island. There were no buildings or people, no pleasure boats to smudge the umblemished line of the distant horizon. A strong southwest wind rippled the surface of the crystal blue water and tempered the heat of the midday sun.

Chiun walked to the edge of the water, glanced over his shoulder to make sure that Remo was watching, then stepped toward the frothy bubbles of the spent surf. As he took his first step, he began to wave his arms back and forth alongside his body, his fingernails pointed downward.

He walked out five steps, his arms still moving, then five more. Then he turned and walked back and stood before Remo.

"Well?" he said.

"That's the lesson for today?" Remo said. "Watching you take a walk in the water?"

"No, the lesson for today is the same as the

lesson for every day: that you are truly an idiot. You saw me walk into the water?"

"Of course. I told you I was paying attention."

"Then look at my sandals," Chiun said. He raised one thin yellow leg toward Remo. His thin yellow shin peeked out from under the lifted edge of his dark red kimono.

Remo looked at the offered sandal, then leaned over to touch it. It was dry, bone dry. And yet he had just seen Chiun walk ten paces out into the ocean.

"How'd you do that?"

"If you were truly paying attention, you would know the answer," Chiun said. "Now this time, watch again. But with your eyes and mind open and your mouth closed, please."

Chiun repeated the stroll into the water and this time Remo saw that the back-and-forth motion of Chiun's arms at the sides of his body was setting up a pressure wall that literally pushed back the water from alongside him.

When Chiun came back, he said, "Did you see?"

"I certainly did," Remo said. "Do you know that Moses did that and he got five books in the Bible?"

To Chiun's unamused look, he quickly added, "Okay, Chiun, I liked it a lot. It was real nice."

"Nice?" Chiun shrieked. "A walk in a garden is nice. A cup of warm tea is nice. Clean underwear is nice. This? This is spectacular." His wispy white hair fluttered in the wind as he shook his head toward Remo.

"All right, Chiun. It's great," Remo said. "It must be terrific at beach parties."

"Do not patronize me, white thing," Chiun said. "This is a tool, not a source of amusement. With this, Wo Lee, the Nearly Great, once escaped an evil king by running through a pond of man-eating fish."

"Hold on. Wo Lee, the Nearly Great?" Remo asked.

"Yes. None other."

"Why was he 'the nearly great'?" Remo asked.

"Because he had the misfortune to select a pupil who did not pay attention."

"All right, enough. I'm paying attention. I just don't see a lot of practical value in being able to part the waters," Remo said.

"I thought it might be particularly helpful to you now that you've taken to loitering in damp caves with strange women," Chiun said. "Now you do it."

Just as Remo walked to the edge of the water, he heard his name called in a soft, pleasantly familiar voice. He turned to see Kim Kiley standing on one of the grass-capped dunes. Her aqua-blue swimsuit emphasized every curve of her full-breasted supple body.

"I've been looking for you everywhere," she said. "What are you two doing over on this side of the island?"

"Nothing," Chiun muttered. "Especially him."

"Let's go swimming then," Kim said with a smile. "The water looks beautiful."

"Good idea," Remo said. "Chiun, I'll practice later. I promise."

"Let us hope that later is not too late," Chiun said.

Kim Kiley said, "I brought a surfboard along. We can take turns on it." She pointed up to the tall saw grass where a long blue-and-white fiberglass board was lying.

"I'll go first," she said. "I want to get the board back by four."

"Go ahead," said Chiun. "You can take my turn too. Also Remo's."

"You're sweet," Kim said.

"Just what I was going to say," Remo agreed.

Kim got the board and launched herself gracefully into the surf. After she cleared the crest of an incoming wave, she jockeyed herself into a sitting position and began to paddle farther out.

"This is impossible," Chiun said. "How can we accomplish anything with all these distractions?"

"This is a vacation," Remo reminded him. "Distractions are what vacations are all about. And anyway, Kim isn't 'all these distractions.' She's the only one."

"It only takes one for you to neglect your training," Chiun said.

Remo's reply was cut short by a cry for help. It was Kim's voice, raised in a thin plaintive wail as the wind carried it across the water. Remo shaded his eyes and spotted her, a tiny speak in the distance. Her head was just above the ocean's surface. Her arms were wrapped around the slippery surface of the board as it bucked and fishtailed, buffeted by the choppy wind-whipped waves.

Remo dived into the surf and swam toward her, his smooth powerful strokes eating up the distance between them. He felt a sense of exhilaration, of breaking free. He had not been able to concentrate during the brief training session; it was all part of that restless feeling that he kept thinking would go away but which he had not been able to shake for the last two weeks. But this, this now felt right.

Raising his head, Remo peered above the white-foamed waves to catch a glimpse of Kim as her hands lost their tentative grip on the board and with one more cry for help, she slipped beneath the surface.

Remo glided across the water now, moving through it not like a man but the way Chiun had taught him, like a fish, being in the water and of it. When he reached the spot where Kim had gone under, he kicked his legs back, twisted and dived. Even this far out, the water was crystal clear.

But he saw no sign of her. Where was she? He started to dive deeper when he felt the slight pressure of movement in the water behind him. He turned, expecting Kim and instead found himself suddenly entangled in a vast net. It closed around, covering him on all sides as if he were some kind of insect who had mistakenly strayed into a spider's waiting web. He struggled to break free, but the more he struggled, the more his twisting body became tangled up in the net. It clung to his arms and legs, and wrapped itself around his body and head. His vision was obscured by the fine, metal-reinforced mesh. Every move he made only bound him tighter.

Remo felt a flash of panic, not for himself but for Kim. She needed him. This was only a net, a simple fisherman's tool, he told himself. Nothing to get worked up about. He would break the net and then continue his search.

Back on the beach, Chiun watched the shadow cast by a ragged-leaf palm tree. Its length told him that two minutes had passed since he had seen Remo's head duck under the waves. Chiun thought he would head back to the condominium soon. It had been a trying day and a cup of tea would be soothing.

Calming himself, concentrating, Remo grasped the net in his hands and felt it slip away. He tried again and again missed. Whipped by the strong current, the fine-meshed webbing kept moving out of reach, and his efforts had only served to draw the net tighter around him. It surrounded him completely now, as tight and clinging as a newly wrapped shroud.

Chiun sighed. He glanced to his right and saw Kim Kiley come running out of the surf and then across the sand back toward her condominium building. Even that woman had sense enough to come in out of the water. It was six minutes now according to the ever-lengthening shadow of the palm tree. Chiun wasn't going to sit here all day while Remo frolicked in the sea. He would wait only a bit longer and then return to the condo alone if Remo didn't get back. If Remo wanted to splash around like a fool all day, that was his business. But Chiun wanted a cup of tea. Was that too much to ask?

Remo felt a tiny trace of light-headedness, the little warning indicator that his thrashing around had begun to use up his air. As the tight-woven netting slipped across his face, he caught a glimpse of a figure in the distance swimming steadily toward him.

Kim, he thought. He had come to save her and now she was going to rescue him.

But as the shadowy figure approached and came into sharper focus, Remo saw that it wasn't Kim. It was a man in frogman's gear.

And he carried a sword in his hand.

* * *

Twelve minutes. Did Remo expect him to loiter around here the entire afternoon like some lavatory attendant hoping for a tip? No. He, Chiun, had better things to do and very soon now, Remo or no Remo, he would depart to do them. He could almost smell the fragrant aroma of fresh tea.

The frogman circled Remo, maneuvering for position. The clear blue water rippled as the thin blade struck out. It poked through the net, straight at Remo's unprotected chest. Remo threw himself sideways, barely out of its path as the blade passed within a quarter-inch of slicing open his rib cage.

The frogman withdrew the blade and quickly struck again. Remo whooshed out of the way but not quickly enough and this time the razor-honed blade had nicked his shoulder. It was nothing more than a scratch but there was a little blood and sooner or later it would draw the sharks.

This was not, Remo decided, such a great vacation after all.

Both hands on the sword this time, the frogman lunged at Remo from above. Fighting the constrictions of the net, Remo fell backward. He could feel the cold smooth steel, even colder than the water, as it passed over his cheekbone like a lover's caress, a foretaste of what was soon to come. He knew he could not last much longer. His head felt as light as a circus balloon.

When he had to, Remo could live on the oxygen stored in his body for hours. But that required stillness, a shutting-down of the body's oxygen needs. He was not able to do that here because of the frogman's attack and he felt a tingle in the lower part of his lungs. How long had he been underwater? It seemed a lifetime. No. Nineteen minutes. He could hang on, he told himself grimly.

Twenty minutes and Chiun couldn't understand what was keeping Remo. Maybe he had slipped out of the water without Chiun seeing him; maybe he was back at the condo, already having put the tea water on to boil.

Remo twisted his body but the blade nicked him again. It had taken almost all his strength to avoid a direct hit, and the net continued to draw tighter around him, restricting his movements further. His lungs were ready to burst; his head was filled with white light. It would all be over soon. He could see the frogman's carnivorous grin, distorted by the Plexiglas face mask. Remo had always wondered what death would look like when he finally met it face to face. He had never expected that it would be an idiot's grin under glass.

The frogman yanked the blade free of the mesh and raised it once more. Remo tried to will his body to move, but nothing happened. His body wasn't listening to him anymore. It knew when to give up. You give up when there is no more air left; you give up when there is no more strength left to fight. Your mind might tell you other things, but your body always knew when it was time to surrender.

It was all over. *Good-bye, Chiun.*

The long slender blade flashed through the water. Remo stayed motionless, his mind already accepting the steel, anticipating the first contact as it sliced through layers of flesh and muscle to burst the fragile bubble of his heart.

As the blade pierced the netting, a yellow hand streaked bubbling through the water, the extended forefinger poking a hole in the frogman's throat. Red bubbles gushed toward the surface like pink champagne as the sword slipped from the frogman's grasp and he sank, limp and lifeless, toward the bottom of the sea.

Remo felt strong hands grasp the net and simply yank it apart. Then he was being pulled upward. His head broke the surface and his lungs greedily gulped in deep drafts of sweet, salt-scented air.

"Always nice to see a friendly face," he said.

"Do you know how long you kept me waiting?" Chiun asked. "And this kimono is ruined. This awful water smell will never leave it."

"Where's Kim?" Remo asked, suddenly panicked.

"She is all right. She had the sense to come out

of the water before the games started," Chiun said.

"How did you know I was in trouble?"

"One can always expect you to be in trouble," Chiun said. He brought his hand up from under the water. The long slender blade of the sword glittered in the sunlight. Chiun's dark eyes narrowed as he read the simple inscription etched on the blade just below the handle. It consisted of only two words, the ancient Indonesian symbols for "Wo" and "son."

As they walked out of the water onto the shore, Remo said, "Little Father, I think I'm better now. I think the hiding time is over."

"Good," said Chiun. "Because it is time that I told you of the Master Who Failed."

Chapter Twelve

After Chiun brewed tea and Remo put on a dry T-shirt and chinos, they sat facing each other, cross-legged on the floor. It was late now and the setting sun filled the airy room with a warm glow.

"I tried to tell you this story the other day but you did not listen."

"Is this the one about the guy who didn't get paid?" Remo asked.

"You might say that," Chiun allowed.

"See? I *was* listening. I told you. I always listen."

"If you always listen, why don't you ever learn anything?" Chiun asked.

"Just lucky, I guess," Remo said with a grin. It felt good to be back; good to be Remo again.

"The prince of whom I spoke was Wo and he had a brother with his eye on the throne, a brother massing a large army far greater than he needed to defend his own lands."

"This sounds like where we come in," Remo said.

"It is, but not if you keep interrupting." He glared at Remo and took a sip of tea. "Prince Wo wished to rid himself of this scheming brother and yet did not wish to have the death laid at his own doorstep, so Prince Wo sent for Master Pak and a bargain was struck. The very next day, the Prince's brother died, by falling from the parapets of his own castle."

"And when the assassin came to be paid?" Remo said.

"He was dismissed. Prince Wo insisted that his brother's death had been a true accident and he would not acknowledge the Master's work. He refused to pay the tribute that was agreed upon."

"This is getting interesting," Remo said, trying to please Chiun.

"It is getting long because you keep interrupting me. Anyway, the following morning the prince's concubine was found dead. The news and manner of her death spread quickly throughout the kingdom and soon everyone knew that the prince's brother had not died by accident. Master Pak had sent his message. He wanted to be paid."

"It's a great way to send a message," Remo said. "A lot more zip than Federal Express. And the prince still refused to pay?"

"No," said Chiun. His thin lips turned up in a wintry smile. "Prince Wo realized his error at once and sent a courier to the assassin with double the payment, one part for the assassination and another to ensure Master Pak's silence."

"All that extra gold. Sounds like a happy ending to me. They must have broken out the party hats back in that mudhole by the bay."

"What mudhole?" Chiun asked.

"Sinanju," Remo explained.

"Silence, you nincompoop," Chiun snapped. "The payment was only part of it. More important than the payment is the manner in which it is made. Prince Wo did not wish to be seen by his subjects as having been forced to pay the assassin, but Master Pak could not let this happen. If one prince refused to pay him, others might try the same. It was no longer enough to be paid; he had to be paid publicly, in tribute, as was his right."

"So he sent the gold back," Remo said.

"Of course not."

"Right."

"He sent back the empty sacks requesting that they be filled again and payment made again where all could see it. Prince Wo refused, for his own pride was so great that he did not wish to be seen bending to any man's will. Instead, he summoned his warriors and mobilized an entire army to pursue and kill a single man."

"I bet it didn't work," Remo said.

"It did not. Prince Wo's oldest and wisest general devised a plan called the seven-sided death. Each manner of death was inscribed on a separate stone. Death by sword, by fire and so forth. But none of the ways worked and Prince Wo's army was decimated and each of the first six stones was shattered.

"The great army had dwindled down to a handful of men and the only way left was that of the seventh stone. It was said to be ultimate, invincible, the one way that would work when all the others had failed."

"So that's why Pak is known as the Master Who Failed?"

"No, that's not why. The seventh stone was never used. Prince Wo and his remaining followers put out to sea and finally disappeared from the known world. And when they vanished, the seventh stone vanished with them."

"Well, what happened to Pak?" Remo asked.

Chiun sighed. "He spent the rest of his days searching for Prince Wo. Finally he was so overcome by disgrace and his own inability to find the prince that he retired to a cave and took no food or water until finally he died. He had a vision though in the very last moments of his life. He foresaw a future time when the descendants of Wo would try to wreak vengeance on another Master of Sinanju. With his dying breath, Pak left a cryptic message, a warning that the seventh stone spoke truth."

He looked up to Remo for comment. Remo shrugged. "Interesting story but that's two thousand years ago. Maybe they wanted to get even once, but, come on, it's a long time ago."

"As long as the bloodline flows unbroken, the memory does not die," Chiun said. He drained his teacup. "Remember when we first came down here? That little article you told me about, the one that described the big stone that they had dug up on this island?"

"I remember mentioning it," Remo said. "Are you telling me that was the seventh stone?"

"It may be," Chiun answered solemnly. "Emperor Smith has pictures of it and he is trying to find out what it says."

"Hold on, Chiun," said Remo. "You speak every language I ever heard of. You can't read this writing?"

"The language is long dead," Chiun said, "and Pak left no instructions in its use."

"It's probably not the same stone at all," Remo said.

"It probably is," Chiun said. "Here is proof." He held up the sword he had taken from the frogman and ran his fingertips over the etching on the blade. "In ancient Indonesian, this says 'Wo' and 'son.' I think the men of the seventh stone are after us."

"And Pak says the seventh stone knows the true way to kill us?" Remo asked.

"So says the legend," Chiun said.

"Then we'd better hope that Smitty finds out what the stone says," Remo said.

"That would be nice," Chiun said agreeably, as he finished his tea.

Chapter Thirteen

Harold W. Smith sat in front of the computer watching the little lights blink on and off as if someone inside the silent machine was trying to send him a message in code.

Smith loved the computer because it was able to do in seconds or minutes what might take humans days and months. But he hated it too because once it started working, there was nothing to do but sit and wait for it to finish. That made him feel guilty. Technically he might be working, but he really wasn't doing anything at all, except drumming his fingers on the console. After too many years with the government, he still got anxiety pains from not working, a tight little knot in his stomach that felt as if he'd swallowed a hard rubber ball.

He headed his own organization and was answerable to no one but the President himself. Yet he had a recurring nightmare, a dread dream of a day when someone would breeze into the CURE headquarters in Rye, New York, look at him, point a finger and say: "There you are, Smith. Goofing off at the computer again."

He felt a slight loosening of the knot in his stomach as a message took form on the computer's monitor screen. The machine had managed to decipher the first part of the message on the stone found in Little Exuma, although why Chiun thought it was important was beyond Smith.

"The two plums," the computer tapped out. Smith said it aloud just to hear the sound of it, but it sounded no better than it read. That was the trouble with ancient languages. They tended to relate things in terms of fruit and stars and trees and birds and entrails. Everything meant something else because the ancients lacked the gift for direct prose.

The machine had hesitated but now it tapped out two words from the end of the inscription. He now had:

"The two plums . . . are bereft."

Not exactly enlightening, Smith thought with a frown. Without the middle, the message made no sense at all, and he had a sinking feeling that even when the computer finally figured out the middle part, the message still wouldn't make much sense.

Still he should let Chiun know what the machine had learned so far. He telephoned Little Exuma and Remo answered on the first ring.

"I've got some information for Chiun," Smith

said. "The inscription on a stone he wanted me to translate."

"Terrific. What does it say?" Remo said.

"Well, I don't have the entire inscription yet. Just a sentence and just the beginning and the end. There's some stuff missing from the middle that the computer still has to figure out," Smith said.

"Just give me what you've got so far," Remo said.

Smith cleared his throat. " 'The two plums,' that's the first part. And then there's a blank. 'Are bereft,' that's the last part." Smith listened to fifteen seconds of silence from the other end of the line. "Did you get that, Remo?" he asked finally.

"Yeah. I got it," said Remo. "The two plums are bereft? That's the great message."

"That's what I have so far."

"What does 'bereft' mean?" Remo asked.

"Destitute, saddened, heartbroken," Smith said.

"Good. And what's the 'two plums' about?"

"I don't know," Smith said.

"Gee," Remo said. "Be sure to call us right away, Smitty, if you get any more exciting news like this. Wow, I can't wait to tell Chiun that the two plums are bereft. He'll be real excited."

"I don't really need your sarcasm," Smith said.

"And I don't really need you," Remo said as he hung up.

* * *

It was a wonderful night for a funeral. Overhead the sky was clear, dusted with a million twinkling stars. There was a steady cooling breeze off the ocean, stirring the flowering vines along the garden wall and filling the night air with their lush sweet fragrance. The weatherman had guaranteed no rain and as if he were comforted by this meteorological perfection, the corpse appeared to be smiling.

The vast emerald-green expanse of Reginald Woburn's back lawn was crowded with the gathered descendants of the Wo clan. Clothed in flowing silk robes, leisure suits, loincloths, they filed past the grave of Ree Wok, their fallen kinsman. He had made the ultimate sacrifice, paid the price that can only be paid once. He had died in battle, the only true way for a Wo warrior to die. In every mind was the thought that there was no greater honor, no greater nobility than that which was now Ree Wok's.

The cool night air was filled with wailing, keening, whispered prayers and warbling chants for the safe swift passage of Ree Wok's departed soul, a symphony of grief played on dozens of different linguistic instruments.

Ree Wok's beautifully appointed satinwood coffin was covered by a thick carpet of flowers, some of species so rare that they had never before been seen in the western hemisphere.

Other descendants of Prince Wo left a variety

of objects at the graveside, each a mark of how a great death was honored in their own native culture.

When the last of the mourners had paid their respects and the grave had been filled in, the tall French doors of the mansion parted and Reginald Woburn III emerged atop a sleek black stallion, its head capped by a coronet of three fluttering plumes, its glistening flanks festooned with jewel-encrusted ribbons.

Reggie said nothing. He looked not right or left. All the kinsmen of Prince Wo could see the grave, solemn set of his handsome features and they knew that for this one moment they did not exist for Reginald Woburn III. Each was sure that his grieving was so pure, so intense that his mind held no room for any other thing. In his overwhelming despair, they knew his soul was as one with that of his departed brother, Ree Wok.

It was a beautiful moment, a time, an event that would live in story and song, a treasured memory passed down from one Wo generation to the next.

Reginald Woburn III gigged the jeweled stallion forward. His face solemn, he rode slowly, regally to the graveside.

Overwhelmed by the magnificent sight, the descendants drew a collective breath. They might speak dozens of different tongues, live dozens of different creeds and cultures, but each at last saw

Reginald Woburn III as a true prince, the true
leader of his flock, heartbroken by the death of
one of his own.

Reggie reached the grave site and carefully
backed the noble stallion up so that the animal
was standing directly over the rectangle of freshly
turned earth. Only then did he acknowledge the
presence of others. Sitting ramrod straight in the
saddle, he turned his head slowly, his clear blue
eyes sweeping the crowd.

Then he reached out and slapped the horse's
neck.

"Okay, Windy," he yelled. "Do it for Daddy."

There was a loud whooshing sound like a
balloon bursting as the black stallion broke wind.
And then took a long, giant dump atop the grave.
The rancorous smell of the manure overpowered
the sweet scent of the thousands of flowers and
blocked out the delicate smoke of the burning
incense. The odor of the horse excrement hung
heavy on the cool night air, as thick as the smell of
death itself.

"Good boy," Reggie said, clapping the horse's
throat. He glared around and said, "That's how
we reward failure. What the hell good is trying if
you don't succeed? I'm fed up with this family
and all its failures and I'm glad this son of a bitch
is dead and the next one who fails I may just hang
from a tree to rot. Now. Who's going to be next?"

Nobody moved. No one spoke. The silence was
so thick it could have been spread on a cracker.

"Well?" Reggie demanded. "Who's next?"

After a long minute, there was a stirring in the shadows. A beautiful woman emerged, the reflected moonlight silvering her lustrous black hair.

"I will be next," Kim Kiley said quietly.

Reggie smiled. "Why have you finally deigned to join us?"

"I was researching the subject," Kim responded calmly. "I am ready now."

"How will you kill him?" Reggie demanded.

"Is the white man the important target?" Kim asked coolly.

For a moment Reggie was flustered, then said. "No. Of course not. The Korean is the real goal."

"Correct," she said. "You asked how I will kill the white man," and she shook her head. "Not I alone. That way will lead to only more failure. *We* will kill him. All of us."

"In what manner?" Reggie said.

"In the manner described by the stone," Kim said with a smile. "And that will bring the old Korean into our grasp too." She paused and stared directly at Reggie, who fidgeted in his saddle. "It was there all the time," Kim said. "You just had to see it. You see, Remo's only weakness is the old man, Chiun, the Korean. And Chiun's loyalty is to Remo. They are two of a kind. They are the plums of the stone."

"But how do we kill them?" Reggie asked.

"The old man is the first plum," Kim said.

"And the way to kill the first plum . . ." She hesitated and smiled. " . . . is with the second plum."

"And how do we kill the second plum?" Reggie asked.

"With the first plum," Kim said softly.

Chapter Fourteen

"There's something outside the door, Chiun," said Remo.

"Of course there is. All through the night, I heard herds of people throwing things against our front door. I didn't sleep for a second," Chiun grumbled.

"It's only an envelope," Remo said. He turned the buff-colored square of paper over and saw his and Chiun's name written on the front in a bold flowing hand with lots of curlicues and swirls.

The note inside carried a lingering trace of familiar perfume.

Dear Remo,

Sorry about the disappearing act yesterday. But the current finally pulled me and the surfboard back to shore and I wanted to get the board back to the rental place before they charged me overtime. Anyway, I know you're a good swimmer so I knew you were safe. But I still feel bad about leaving you without a word, so to make up for it, I'd like to invite you to a party. It's a kind of family reunion that my people are having. It starts at two this afternoon at the Woburn estate on the northern tip of the island. Please bring Chiun along too. I've told everyone so much about you two and the family is very anxious to meet you both. There'll be a special surprise.

Love, Kim

Chiun padded out of the bedroom and saw Remo in the doorway reading the note.

"Are you finished reading my mail?" Chiun asked.

"What makes you think it's for you?"

"Who would write anything to you?" Chiun said. He snatched the note from Remo's hands and read it slowly.

"It's from Kim," Remo said. "An invitation to a party."

"I can see that for myself. I remember you took me to a party once and people kept trying to get me to eat vile things that were piled up on crackers and buy plastic bowls with lids on them. Do you think this will be that kind of a party?"

"I don't think so," Remo said.

"Wait. Hold. A special surprise, she says," said Chiun.

"Right."

"What is that?" Chiun asked.

"I don't know. If I knew, it wouldn't be a surprise," Remo said.

"It's Barbra Streisand," Chiun said. "I know it. This Kim person has been feeling guilty because she has been keeping you away from your training and now she is going to present me with Barbra Streisand to make amends."

"I don't think any party you're likely to go to is going to make you a gift of Barbra Streisand," Remo said.

"We are going," Chiun said with finality. "I will wear my new robes. Do you want one of my old robes to wear?"

"No, thank you."

"What *are* you going to wear?"

"A black T-shirt and black pants," Remo said. "Casual, yet restrained. A perfect complement for every occasion."

"You have no imagination," Chiun said.

"Yes I do," Remo said. "Today I'm thinking about wearing socks."

"I'm sure all will be impressed," Chiun said.

"Nothing's too good for Barbra Streisand," Remo said.

They left to walk to the party but were only a few yards along the beach when the telephone back in their condo rang.

"I'll get it," Remo said, turning back toward the front door.

"Get what?"

"The phone," Remo called back.

"Just don't bring it back with you," Chiun said. "I hate those things."

Smith was on the other end of the line. "I have it," he told Remo. "The whole inscription."

"What is it?" Remo said.

"The first part seems to be a listing of weapons. It talks about using spears and fire and the sea and finally it says to use time. It talks about a special killer. Does that mean anything to you?"

"No, but maybe to Chiun. Anything else?"

"But the rest of it, that missing section?"

"Yes?" Remo said.

"The missing word is 'cleaved.' "

"Cleaved?" said Remo.

"Right. Split. Broken. The inscription reads: 'The two plums, cleaved, are bereft.'" He sounded proud.

"What does it mean though?" Remo asked. "It sounds like some whiny housewife's note to a grocery store. 'The two plums, cleaved, are bereft.' Who cares about broken plums?"

"I don't know," Smith said. "I thought you would."

"Thanks, Smitty. I'll tell Chiun."

When he told Chiun of Smith's report, the old Korean seemed more interested in the listing of weapons.

"You say the last one on the list was time?" Chiun asked.

"That's what Smith said. What kind of a weapon is time?" Remo asked.

"The most dangerous of all," Chiun said.

"How's that?"

"If one waits long enough, his enemy will think he has forgotten and relax his guard."

"So you think this was really from the seventh stone of Prince Wo?" asked Remo.

Chiun nodded silently.

"And what is that about 'The two plums, cleaved, are bereft'?" Remo asked.

"I think we will find out soon," Chiun said.

The rolling lawns of the Worburn estate looked like the site for the annual Christmas picnic of the United Nations. People in every form of native garb Remo had ever seen milled about. They moved aside silently to let Remo and Chiun pass, then closed up behind them. The sounds of un-translated whispers followed them across the green field.

Remo counted ten long tables draped in white damask and laden with all kinds of food and drink. The mingled aromas of curry, fish and meat competed with steaming cabbage and spicy Indonesian lamb. There were steam tables of vegetables and bowls of fresh fruit, many that Remo had never seen before.

"This place smells like a Bombay alley," Chiun said, his nose wrinkling in disgust.

Remo pointed ahead of them. There was a small linen-covered table. Atop it was a silver pitcher of fresh water and a silver chafing dish heaped to the top with clumpy, mushlike rice.

"For us," Remo said. He thought it was nice of Kim Kiley to remember and he wondered where she was.

He looked but could not see her in the crowd. She had said this was a family reunion and he had expected a couple of dozen people in leisure suits, shorts and funny straw hats, clustered around a barbecue grill. He hadn't expected this.

"I don't see Barbra Streisand," Chiun said.

"Maybe she's going to ride in on an elephant," Remo said.

A man in tweeds stepped up and offered his hand to Remo. "So very glad you could come," he said. "I'm Rutherford Wobley." He nodded politely to Chiun as Remo shook his hand.

"And this is Ruddy Woczneczk," he said. Remo went through the process again with a moon-faced Slav.

"Lee Wotan," the Oriental next to him said and bowed. "And these are . . ." He began to rattle off the names of people standing near. Wofton, Woworth, Wosento and Wopo. All the names sounded alike to Remo and he nodded and smiled and as soon as he could slipped away into the crowd.

The names, he thought. Why did every one of them start with W-O? And it wasn't just the people he'd met this afternoon. There were William and Ethel Wonder, the film people, and Jim Worthman, their photographer. And what about the fanatical Indonesian who tried to kill the President? His name had been Du Wok. It seemed to Remo that everywhere he had gone in the last few weeks, he had run into people whose names began with W-O.

With one bright, shining exception.

Remo sauntered up the bright lawn toward the house. He had left Chiun behind, in animated conversation with a young aristocratic man dressed in an impeccable white linen suit. It seemed that he and Chiun had met on the island before because they were talking like old friends.

Nearer the house was a series of reflecting pools strewn with water lilies and a large latticework gazebo.

Next to the house he saw four towering columns, like flagpoles, each of them topped with a cluster of rectangles covered completely with dark cloths.

He slipped into the house and found a telephone in the library. Smith answered on the first ring.

"Look up a name for me," Remo said. "Kim Kiley."

"The movie actress?" Smith asked.

"That's the one."

"Hold on." Smith put the telephone down and Remo heard the click of buttons being pushed and then a muted whirring sound. "Here it is," Smith said as he came back on the line. "Kiley, Kimberley. Born Karen Wolinski, 1953. . . ."

"Spell that last name," Remo sid.

"W-o-l-i-n-s-k-i," Smith said.

"Thank you," Remo said. He hung up the telephone and stood there still for a moment, not quite ready to believe it. But it had to be true; there was just too much to be written off as coincidence.

The sounds of the party drifted in through the open window. Laughter, music, the clinking of glasses. But Remo was not in the party mood anymore and he walked out a side door of the mansion and ambled along the beach.

It was all connected somehow. Kim and all the others whose names began with W-O. All the loose threads tied in with the attempts on his life, an ancient stone that spoke the truth, an unbending prince and his descendants and Masters of Sinanju, past and present. They were all bound together by a cord that stretched from this moment back across the centuries. What was it Chiun had said? Remo remembered:

"As long as the bloodline flows unbroken, the memory never dies."

Remo found that his footsteps had carried him to the secluded cove where he and Kim had first made love. That still bothered him. If Kim was a part of some kind of revenge scheme, why had she stayed in the cave with him? They had been making love when the giant wave came crashing in. If she had lured Remo there to kill him, surely she must have realized that she was going to her own death as well. Somehow he didn't believe that.

Kim might be a loyal descendant of Prince Wo but she didn't seem like the kind of woman who would kill herself just to even up a two-thousand-year-old score.

Remo padded into the cave and smiled when he saw the spot where they had lain together on the warm sand. The memory was still vivid, as real as the salt in the sea air.

He wandered back farther into the cavern. He remembered now that when the thundering wall of water had filled the mouth of the cave, Kim hadn't run instinctively toward the entrance. She had turned instead and bolted toward the back of the opening, farther from safety, farther away from the air and the land above.

Remo walked back to the spot where he had scooped her up as she kicked and struck and bit at him. He glanced up and saw a glimmer of light from above. There it was. An opening in the roof of the cave, just big enough for one person to pass through. If a person were standing on this exact spot, the onrush of water would lift him up right to that opening.

No wonder Kim had fought so hard when

Remo grabbed her. He had chalked it up to panic but, in truth, she had been trying to break free to save herself, never considering the possibility that Remo would be able to swim against the onrushing water and carry them both to safety.

Just to make sure, Remo clambered up the rocks and boosted himself through the opening. It was a tight squeeze for him, but it would have been easy for Kim Kiley.

He found himself on a rocky promontory above the cave. Even when the tide was highest, someone standing here would have been safe.

There was nothing to do now but to accept the facts. It had been Kim all along, not caring for him at all, but leading him around like a sacrificial lamb. First the cave and when that had not worked, out into the ocean where the frogman had been waiting to finish him off. And she had probably been tied in with the gunmen too, those at the Indian reservation.

What Remo had thought was an affectionate caring woman had turned out to be nothing more than an attractive piece of bait.

Remo made his way back along the beach, through the mansion and out onto the spacious lawn. The party was in full swing. He saw that Chiun was still talking to that aristocratic man in white, as well as a half-dozen others gathered around in a tight circle.

Remo felt a hand on his shoulder. He turned to

see Kim there, looking heartbreakingly beautiful in a low-cut blue silk dress.

"Darling," she whispered and threw her arms around his neck.

She held Remo tight, pressing against him. His nostrils filled with the scent of the perfume she wore. It was just as he remembered it from the very first day, rich and exotic. Bitterly he told himself: as primitive and powerful as a carved stone on a tropical beach.

She finally released him but the heavy perfume seemed to cling to his clothes like a constant painful reminder of his own vulnerability.

"Are you having a good time?" she asked with a Hollywood dazzler of a smile.

Remo said nothing. He looked at her once more, then turned and started through the crowd to get Chiun.

Chapter Fifteen

He did not see Chiun and the crowd was already surging up the hill toward the mansion. A young tweedy man stepped up next to Remo and nudged him with an elbow.

"The entertainment's about to start."

"I bet," Remo said.

He caught a glimpse of shimmering green and gold that must have come from Chiun's robes and pushed his way through the crowd until he found the aged Korean.

"They don't have Barbra Streisand," Chiun said. "But they're going to have a circus." He sounded happy.

Remo leaned over to whisper so that no one else could hear. "Chiun, these are Prince Wo's descendants. They're our enemies."

Chiun hissed back. "*I* know that."

"Then what are we staying here for? Let's book."

"That means leave?" Chiun asked.

"That means leave," Remo said.

"So we leave and what then?" Chiun asked. "Another day, another year and these people who would not pay their proper bill to Master Pak come to us again? It is better that we resolve all this now."

"If you say so," Remo said.

"I say so," Chiun said. "You go stand on the other side and keep your eyes open."

"Is there a leader? Why not just splatter him now?" Remo said.

"Because we do not know what will happen then. To act without information is to court disaster. The other side."

"All right," Remo said, and moved around onto the other side of the rectangular clearing which was marked at each corner by the large columns he had noticed earlier. The black cloths that covered the tops of the columns were still in place.

The young man whom Chiun had been talking to earlier was now standing in the center of the clearing.

He raised a hand for silence, got it, and announced in a clear voice: "I am Reginald Woburn the Third. I welcome you to the Wo family reunion. Let the fun begin."

As he stepped out of the clearing a brass gong somewhere was struck, sounding a deep-throated reverberation. A trio of high-pitched wood flutes lay down a sweet chord of melody. Cymbals

crashed and the gong boomed again as a troupe of
brightly clad Oriental acrobats came tumbling
through the crowd and into the ring.

"The Amazing Wofans," the young man next to
Remo said.

"If you're going to be my tour director, what's
your name?" Remo asked.

"Rutherford Wobley," the man said.

"I thought so," Remo said.

He looked away in disgust and saw the Wofans
spinning around the ring, doing handsprings and
cartwheels, back flips and rolls. Their bodies flew
through the air like bright blurs of color as they
passed over and under each other like whirling
tops in constant motion. While the area they had
to work in was not large, they managed to sail
through a series of interweaving patterns as
complex as a spider's web made from pure energy
and motion.

The pajama-clad performers grouped in the
center of the ring and flipped themselves upward
to form a human pyramid. They were good,
Remo thought disgustedly, but he'd seen it all
before. He wondered when they were going to
start spinning plates on long bamboo poles.

The athletes dismantled the pyramid, rolling to
the ground, to the applause of the spectators.
Remo glanced across the clearing, looking for
Chiun, but he could not see him.

The high-pitched piping of the flutes filled the
air with a sound like a mournful wail. The

cymbals crashed and then the gong again with its deep lingering echo.

The acrobats responded to the music. They flew across the ring, two, three, four at once, speeding smudges of color that seemed to defy the laws of gravity, tumbling over each other, seeming to pause in the air at the top of their leaps, working their way across the clearing. And then a blue-clad acrobat overshot the rest of the performers and came hurtling at Remo like a dive bomber.

It had started. Remo stepped to the side a half-pace and raised a hand. It looked as if he hadn't really done anything, maybe just waved to someone in the crowd on the other side of the arena. But the acrobat's feetfirst dive missed Remo completely, except where the Oriental's shoulder brushed the tip of Remo's outstretched hand. The contact was punctuated by the snapping sound of breaking bone, a whoosh of exhaled air and then a prolonged scream as the acrobat hit the ground. This time he did not bounce up.

Two more came lunging toward Remo. Red and green this time. Remo turned slightly, catching one with his shoulder blade and the second with his knee. He hoped that Chiun was watching because he felt that his technique was really good on the two moves. The acrobats' bellows of pained surprise drowned out the frantic warbling of the flutes. The red-and-green-

clad men popped skyward like bubbles in a
breeze. Like bubbles, they were broken when
they hit the ground. From the corner of his eye as
he turned, Remo saw Reginald Woburn yank the
cord that dangled from one of the rectangle-
clustered poles. There was a blinding flash of light
as a mirror on the pole picked up and reflected the
brilliant intensity of the sun's glare directly into
Remo's eyes. Remo blinked in surprise. As he
opened his eyes again, he had to ignore the mirror
because the remaining Oriental acrobats were
coming toward him, with knives they had drawn
from inside their clothing. Remo ducked out of
their way and as he did there was another flash of
blinding light. Then another. And another.

The harsh white light seared his eyes. Remo
ducked away from the acrobats, into the crowd of
people standing around the performance arena,
his eyes screwed shut tightly. He opened them
again, but he still could not see. The brightness
had shocked his vision for a moment, and behind
him, he could hear the yelling of the Oriental
acrobats as they tried to get to him.

Remo fled, then stopped as a thin high voice
rose above the sounds of a hundred different
noises. It was Chiun's voice rising above the
crowd. It sounded metallic and strained.

"Remo," Chiun wailed. "Help me. Attack
now. Free me. Help."

His blind eyes burning, Remo lunged toward

the voice. Eight steps he knew would bring him to it. But when he was there, all he felt was stillness. There were people there, poised and waiting. Remo could feel them, hear their breathing, sense the coiled tension in their bodies, feel the small movements they made even when they thought they were standing perfectly still.

But there was nothing in the spot where Chiun's voice had come from.

Behind him, Remo heard the voices of the acrobats moving toward him. And he caught the scent of perfume, a painfully familiar fragrance that stirred up far too many memories. It was Kim Kiley's perfume, rich and exotic, as individual as a fingerprint when it intermingled with the scent of her own body.

She was there and then there was another scent.

It was the smell of the tiny particles of residue that linger in a gun barrel after it has been fired. No matter how many times the gun was cleaned, the smell always remained for those with the ability to sense it.

Remo felt the air change again, heard the whisper of motion as a slender finger pulled backward slowly on a trigger. He wanted to yell "No" but there was no time, and instead his unspoken word turned into a thunderous roar of despair that shattered the stillness as Remo, sightless but unerring, reached out for the sound and brought his hand down on the white fragrant neck. He heard the dry-stick sound of snapping bone.

Behind him, the acrobats were leaping toward him. He could feel the pressure of their bodies moving through the air.

But they never reached him. There was the sound of thump-thump-thump like three heavy stones dropped into a mud puddle. He knew their three bodies had ceased moving.

Suddenly, the air was clamorous with the sound of screams, shrieking and pounding feet as the crowd panicked and ran in all directions.

The searing pain of blindness still burned Remo's eyes. He groped for a moment in a world of white night, until he sensed the tall metal structure nearby. He had to turn off the lights; he had to see again; he had to find Chiun.

On the ground near the pole, Remo found a stone-cut glass tumbler dropped by one of the fleeing guests. He sensed its weight and then tossed it upward in a spiraling arc.

He heard the shattering sound as the glass connected with its target. The mirror atop the pole smashed into a million crystalline fragments that rained down from the sky in a magnificent light show.

The other three lights still blinded him, but then he heard the glass of the lights break—pop, pop, pop—and a sudden darkness descended over the lawn. He blinked once and his vision began to return.

The first thing he saw was Chiun, turning away from having blasted out the three other lights with stones.

"You're all right?" Remo asked.

"All in all, I would have preferred Barbra Streisand," Chiun said.

Remo turned around and saw Kim. She lay next to Reginald Woburn III, the two of them stretched out amid a sea of glittering crystals from the broken light reflectors. To their left were the three last Oriental acrobats, their bodies twisted ungracefully in death.

Kim Kiley's perfect face stared skyward, her eyes masked by a pair of dark glasses. A pistol rested on the curled fingers of her right hand. Remo turned away.

"How did you know to kill her?" asked Chiun.

"I knew," Remo said quietly. "How did you know to kill him?"

"He was the leader; if we are ever to have any peace, he must go."

"You waited long enough," Remo said. "I was stumbling around there, not able to see, and you weren't anywhere."

"I found you though," Chiun said. "I just followed the sound of an ox stomping around and, naturally, it was you."

"I don't understand what they were doing," Remo said.

"They tried to make each of us think that the

other was hurt," Chiun said. "We were their 'two plums.' "

"The two plums, cleaved, were bereft," Remo said.

"Correct. They thought if each of us thought the other was in danger, we would lower our defenses and become vulnerable," Chiun said.

"And you weren't hurt? You weren't in any danger?"

"Of course not," Chiun said disdainfully. He leaned over and picked up the fragments of a small black box. "It was some mechanical device, one of those tape-recorder things that does not record a television picture but only noise. I stepped on it when the unrecognizable screeching from it became unbearable."

"So we weren't cleaved and we aren't bereft," Remo said.

"As if any group of barbarians could cleave the House of Sinanju," Chiun said.

Both men paused to look around. The lawns were empty as far as the eye could see. The family of Wo had scattered.

Chapter Sixteen

"All's well that ends well," Remo said when they were back in the condominium.

"Nothing has ended," Chiun said.

"What do you mean? Woburn's dead; the family took off for the hills, what's left?"

"The House of Wo owes the House of Sinanju a public apology."

"Chiun, drop it," said Remo. "It's two thousand years old."

"A debt is a debt."

Chiun was standing by the window, looking out over the ocean. "There is already a new prince of the House of Wo. Let us hope he has the wisdom his predecessors had not."

Chiun stayed by the window until well after dark. Then Remo heard him move toward the front door. He heard the door open and a few whispered words and when he came back into the living room, Chiun was holding an envelope.

The old Korean opened it and read the message.

"It is an invitation," he said.

"You go. My dance card's filled," Remo said.

"It is an invitation for the House of Sinanju to meet with the House of Wo. We will both go."

"I'm part of the House of Sinanju?" Remo said.

Chiun looked up with an innocent expression. "Of course you are," he said.

"Thank you," said Remo.

"'Every house must have a cellar," Chiun said. "Heh, heh. You're the cellar of the House of Sinanju. Heh, heh. The cellar. Heh, heh."

They left at daybreak. Chiun wore a white-and-black ceremonial robe that Remo had never seen before. Emblazoned across the shoulders, in delicate silken embroidery, was a Korean character that Remo recognized as the symbol of the House of Sinanju. It translated as "center" and it meant that the House of Sinanju was the center of the world.

As the two men neared the porticoed front entrance to the sprawling mansion, the arched front doors swung open and four men emerged bearing two stretchers, which held the bodies of Reginald Woburn and Kim Kiley. Remo looked away as they passed and then back again as the island constable followed behind them.

"Ain't no morder," the constable muttered to himself. "Dat's for sure. No arrow in the heart, they be natural causes."

Remo and Chiun entered the mansion. Eerie silence testified that it was empty and Remo said, "I think maybe they're up to something. I don't trust them."

"We shall see," Chiun said quietly. "I am the Master of Sinanju and you are the next Master. This business with the Wos has gone on for too many years now. This day will see it end."

"Sure," Remo said. "We'll kill them all. What's a little carnage as long as it settles a score that nobody's old enough to remember?"

He followed Chiun through the house and then out the front entrance. There, awaiting them on the front lawn, were all the living descendants of Prince Wo. Remo scanned the rows of solemn faces, red, black, yellow, white and brown. No one was smiling.

"Who said big families had more fun?" Remo muttered.

Chiun walked down the steps, his silken robe swirling about him. He halted a few feet from the front rank of men and inclined his head slightly, the smallest of small bows.

"I am Chiun, Master of Sinanju," he said magisterially. "This is Remo, heir to the House of Sinanju. We are here."

A plump Oriental man dressed in a simple crimson robe stepped out of the front rank and bowed to Chiun. "I am Lee Wofan," he said solemnly. "The new prince in the long and illustrious line of the great Prince Wo. I have asked you here to discuss a matter of tribute."

"A tribute denied my predecessor, Master Pak," Chiun said.

"A tribute withheld by Prince Wo as a sign that showed the power of his rule," Lee Wofan said softly.

"And for his arrogance and pride," Chiun said, "Master Pak, one lone man, banished a prince and his army and his court from the face of the civilized world."

"It is so," Wofan agreed. "Here. To this very island Prince Wo came."

There was a sweet sadness in Chiun's voice as he spoke again. "And it was only for words," he said. "A public acknowledgment that the prince recognized Master Pak's performance of his contract." He paused for a moment. The silence was absolute. "And because of that, so many have died," Chiun said.

"It is as you say," Lee Wofan said. "Our legacy has been a curse from Prince Wo the Wanderer. This curse has followed my family in all its branches for two thousand years. Now the curse will be lifted. For we, the family of Wo, now do publicly acclaim the work of the great Master Pak in aiding our ancestor Prince Wo. And we further affirm that the Masters of Sinanju are assassins without equal. In this age or any other."

Chiun bowed his deepest bow. "I, Chiun, reigning Master of the House of Sinanju, accept your tribute for myself and for all Masters, past, present, and yet to come."

"Accept it and more," said Lee Wofan. He stepped to one side and then all the gathered descendants of Wo parted to reveal the stone itself, the stone whose message—to wait until the House of Sinanju had two heads and then to separate and kill them—had failed and brought only more death to the House of Wo.

"Our feud is ended," Lee Wofan said. "Never again will we heed the words written on this stone. We wish to live in peace."

Chiun turned to smile at Remo, then walked through the crowd until he faced the stone.

His voice raised above the crowd, he intoned: "So be our conflict behind us. But never forget Prince Wo or his legend or the Masters of Sinanju who will from this time forward be your friends and allies in trouble. Go back to your lands and remember. For it is only through our memories that the greatness of the past lives on."

With that, Chiun thrust out his hand. Once, twice, thrice. The stone shattered into a million pieces that streaked skyward, wheeling and dancing, crystal bright under the rising sun.

"Welcome home, children of Wo," Chiun said, then turned and walked off through the crowd.

They dropped to their knees as he passed among them.

Exciting Reading from SIGNET

(0451)

☐ **THE SPECIALIST #1: A TALENT FOR REVENGE** by John Cutter.
(127994—$2.25)*

☐ **THE SPECIALIST #2: MANHATTAN REVENGE** by John Cutter.
(128001—$2.25)*

☐ **THE SPECIALIST #3: SULLIVAN'S REVENGE** by John Cutter.
(130499—$2.25)*

☐ **THE SPECIALIST #4: THE PSYCHO SOLDIERS** by John Cutter.
(131053—$2.25)*

☐ **THE SPECIALIST #5: THE MALTESE VENGEANCE** by John Cutter.
(131924—$2.25)*

☐ **THE SPECIALIST #6: THE BIG ONE** by John Cutter. (132726—$2.25)*

☐ **THE SPECIALIST #7: THE VENDETTA** by John Cutter. (134036—$2.50)

☐ **THE SPECIALIST #8: ONE-MAN ARMY** by John Cutter. (135180—$2.50)

☐ **THE DESTROYER #59: THE ARMS OF KALI** by Warren Murphy and Richard
Sapir. (132416—$2.95)*

☐ **THE DESTROYER #60: THE END OF THE GAME** by Warren Murphy and
Richard Sapir. (133986—$2.95)*

☐ **THE DESTROYER #61: LORDS OF THE EARTH** by Warren Murphy and
Richard Sapir. (135601—$2.95)*

☐ **THE VIKING CIPHER #1: ICEBOUND** by Rick Spencer.
(125460—$2.50)*

☐ **THE VIKING CIPHER #2: ALL THAT GLITTERS** by Rick Spencer.
(125479—$2.50)*

☐ **THE VIKING CIPHER #3: THE MONEYMASTER** by Rick Spencer.
(127579—$2.50)*

☐ **THE VIKING CIPHER #4: THE TERROR MERCHANT** by Rick Spencer.
(129024—$2.50)*

☐ **THE VIKING CIPHER #5: THE DEVIL'S MIRROR** by Rick Spencer.
(131045—$2.50)*

*Price is slightly higher in Canada

Buy them at your local bookstore or use this convenient coupon for ordering.
NEW AMERICAN LIBRARY,
P.O. Box 999, Bergenfield, New Jersey 07621
Please send me the books I have checked above. I am enclosing $_____
(please add $1.00 to this order to cover postage and handling). Send check
or money order—no cash or C.O.D.'s. Prices and numbers are subject to change
without notice.
Name_____
Address_____
City_____State_____Zip Code_____
Allow 4-6 weeks for delivery.
This offer is subject to withdrawal without notice.